DUKE'S DEN

DUKE'S DEN

Becky Citra

ORCA BOOK PUBLISHERS

Library and Archives Canada Cataloguing in Publication

Citra, Becky, author
Duke's den / Becky Citra.

Issued in print and electronic formats.
ISBN 978-1-4598-0901-7 (pbk.).—ISBN 978-1-4598-0902-4 (pdf).—
ISBN 978-1-4598-0903-1 (epub)

I. Title.
PS8555.I87D83 2016   jc813'.54   C2015-904490-1
C2015-904491-X

First published in the United States, 2016
Library of Congress Control Number: 2015946328

Summary: In this middle-grade novel, Amelia finds a renewed sense
of belonging when Duke, Gabriella and their menagerie of exotic
rescued animals move into the apartment downstairs.

*Orca Book Publishers is dedicated to preserving the environment and
has printed this book on Forest Stewardship Council® certified paper.*

Orca Book Publishers gratefully acknowledges the support for its publishing
programs provided by the following agencies: the Government of Canada through the
Canada Book Fund and the Canada Council for the Arts, and the Province of British
Columbia through the BC Arts Council and the Book Publishing Tax Credit.

Cover design by Teresa Bubela
Cover artwork by Monika Melnychuk

www.orcabook.com
Printed and bound in Canada.

19   18   17   16   •   4   3   2   1

To Michael, Bianca and Xander

ONE

ONE

A melia saw everything through the slats of her bedroom blind. A rust-speckled blue van crept up the street and rattled to a stop in front of their house. She crossed her fingers. *Please, please, please, make everything go right.*

The front door of the van sprang open, and a guy with glasses and a mop of curly brown hair leaped out. He peered at a paper in his hand, glanced up at the house and then stared at his watch.

He must be Duke, Amelia decided. But where was Gabriella?

The guy got back in the van, but he left the door open, and hip-hop music drifted up through Amelia's open window. Then, in the distance, a roaring sound grew louder and louder, drowning out the hip-hop. A silver motorcycle raced down the street. It swerved behind the van, and two people wearing black leather coats and pants and matching purple helmets scrambled off. One of them was very tall, the other much shorter. Was the tall guy Duke and the guy in the van someone else? Amelia chewed her bottom lip. Tall could be a problem. The short person tugged off her helmet, and red hair cascaded to her waist. Gabriella for sure!

They were talking to the driver of the van now, who had gotten back out. Then the guy from the motorcycle gestured with his arm, and they disappeared around the side of the house.

Amelia grabbed the key from her dresser and sped down the hall. The door to the downstairs apartment was at the back of the house, down three concrete stairs. The tall guy from the motorcycle was rattling the doorknob. He'd taken off his helmet, and he had a buzz cut. Up close, he was even bigger. Gabriella peered through the narrow window, and the van driver stared at his watch again and said, "I've got other things to do today, you know."

"Hi," Amelia said. "I'm Amelia. I live upstairs."

Gabriella gave her a dazzling smile. "I am Gabriella, and this is Duke, and this is Duke's brother, Simon." She shook Amelia's hand. "*Enchantée*."

Duke *was* the tall guy!

"Gabriella's French," Duke explained, rattling the doorknob again.

"Parisienne." Gabriella flashed another of her megawatt smiles.

Amelia loved the sound of that. *Parisienne*. And she loved the way Gabriella said her *r*'s and the way *brother* sounded like *bruder*. She would have beamed back, but she had broken off the tip of her front tooth running into a pole in the school playground, and she looked like a pirate.

"I thought there was supposed to be a key under some pot," Simon said. "Does anyone know where it is? Or is that too much to ask?"

Amelia produced the key.

The door opened directly into the kitchen, which was crowded with four people. Amelia's mom, Diane, had furnished the apartment with bits and pieces she had picked up from secondhand stores. She had also opened all the curtains so the apartment would look as bright as possible for a basement suite.

Before Amelia could shout a warning, Duke headed to the living room.

Crack! His head slammed into the top of the doorway.

"Ouch!" Amelia said.

Gabriella winced. "*Merde!*"

"The doorways are…um…a little low," Amelia said.

Duke rubbed his forehead and gazed up. "The ceilings are a little low too. Not much clearance there. Maybe half an inch."

But he didn't sound mad. "I'll try that again," he said as he crab-walked into the living room. "It looks good in here," he called back. "It'll be fine."

Amelia felt like she'd been holding her breath all day. Duke and Gabriella had taken the apartment sight unseen, which was risky. Six different sets of people had viewed it and turned it down in the last week. One person said it would be great for a family of hobbits.

The tour of the apartment took only a few minutes. A kitchen, a living room, a narrow hallway with two bedrooms and a bathroom. Amelia stood behind Duke and Gabriella while they inspected the smallest bedroom, which was empty.

"We ran out of furniture," Amelia started to explain, but she could tell Duke wasn't listening. He was counting the number of electrical sockets. She was sure she heard him mumble to Gabriella, "Perfect for Winston," and then she decided she'd made a mistake. Her mom had said they had no kids. And who would name a kid Winston anyway?

Simon appeared in the doorway with a box. "Could use some help!" he growled.

They trekked back and forth to the van. Cardboard boxes, baskets and bags overflowing with clothes piled up on the kitchen floor.

Amelia kept sneaking peeks at Gabriella. Her bright-red hair was amazing. Her skin was almost white, and she wore lots of black mascara and eyeliner and smelled like vanilla. She had a tiny green lizard tattooed on her shoulder.

Gabriella chattered while they unpacked dishes from a carton. "We will come up tonight to meet your parents."

"My mom," Amelia said.

"Parents split up?"

Amelia nodded.

Gabriella's brown eyes filled with sympathy. "Men!" She leaned toward Amelia and whispered, "Duke is an angel, but he drives me crazy."

"There's no more room in the cupboards," Amelia said, changing the subject. "And there's still lots more stuff."

"It doesn't matter. We can leave some of it in boxes."

Duke and Simon hauled in a freezer chest, sealed shut with duct tape. "We'll unpack this one later," Duke said.

"I'm off now," Simon said. "I'll take these empty boxes and get the rest later. What time are you coming tonight?"

Duke fired a definite warning look at Simon. Amelia intercepted it. She stopped wondering what was in the freezer chest and pretended to be busy stuffing crumpled newspaper into a garbage bag. She perked up her ears.

"Midnight," Duke said in a low voice.

At least, that's what Amelia thought he might have said. Duke was mumbling again and it sounded more like, "Mmmnnnat."

So. Duke was going somewhere at midnight, *maybe*. What made it really interesting was that he didn't want Amelia to know.

She tied the garbage bag shut.

Somehow she had to find out what was going on.

TWO

It was Amelia's night to make supper. Salad and leftover grilled chicken. Her mom had been on a diet, on and off, since she'd seen Candice at the hockey game the night she and Amelia went to watch the Canucks.

Candice was Amelia's dad's new wife. Well, not *wife*—they weren't married yet, but they might as well be. *"He calls her Candy. Can you believe it?"* Diane had said incredulously. *"She's had twins, for God's sake, and now another baby, and she must be a size six!"*

"Who cares, Mom?" Amelia thought her mom looked good. Maybe a little bit like she was squeezed into those new jeans she'd bought, but she had gorgeous honey-colored hair and great skin. Amelia always loved it when people told her she looked like her mom, even though it wasn't totally true. Amelia's hair was ordinary brown, and lately she'd noticed blackheads on her nose.

This was one of the weeks when Diane was on a diet. Amelia rinsed the lettuce and chopped tomatoes, cucumbers, red peppers and carrots. She put the salad in the fridge, grabbed her backpack and flopped down in the living room in front of the TV.

She spread out her homework on the coffee table, a page of long division and a paragraph for language arts that answered the questions Who? What? When? Where? and Why? She decided to write about a guy on Dr. Phil who cheated on his wife. The Why? was the hardest part. She set to work, and after one rerun of *Family Guy* and one episode of *Dragon's Den*, she was done.

She heard her mom at the front door and hopped up to help her. Grocery bags dangled from Diane's arms. Strands of hair had escaped from her ponytail, and her tan looked faded.

Diane let the bags slide to the floor. "Well?"

"They like it."

"Bingo." Diane grinned.

Amelia grinned back.

Diane's smile evaporated. "Your tooth! Oh God, sweetie, I forgot to phone the dentist."

"Mom, Gabriella's from Paris!"

"Tell me all about it while we eat. I'm famished."

✿ ✿ ✿

Before they dug into the salad, they raised their glasses of apple juice and clinked them together.

"To Great-Aunt Mildred," Diane said.

They always toasted Great-Aunt Mildred at supper. Great-Aunt Mildred (Diane's father's aunt) had died the summer before and left her house to Diane. *Fortuitous timing*, Diane had said after she got over feeling guilty (she had never visited the old lady and had actually thought she'd died years earlier). No one knew why Mildred had left her house to Diane, but she had. The house had a tiny mortgage that Diane's job at Miss Jane's was just enough to cover.

The house was okay, but it was nothing like their old place—a heritage house on the west side of Vancouver. *Heritage* meant that it was old but in a beautiful way, with real oak beams, hardwood floors, leaded stained-glass windows and a fireplace mantel carved by someone famous.

Now Candice's seven-year-old twins, Kelsey and Kaitlin, were in Amelia's old room, and the den had been turned into a nursery for the new baby, Sam. Amelia had never been back to her house, not once. She refused, even on Christmas Eve when "Candy" invited her to help make cookies for Santa with the girls and open presents.

Great-Aunt Mildred's house was a bungalow on the east side of Vancouver. It was old too—"post-war stucco," Diane called it—but there was nothing about it that you would want to preserve. It had linoleum in the kitchen, beige wall-to-wall carpet in the living room, and tiny square pink tiles in the bathroom, which Diane said were "very retro." The best thing about it was the apartment in the basement.

The doorbell rang when they got to dessert—gluten-free chocolate-chip cookies from a bakery on Hastings Street.

It was Duke and Gabriella. Amelia made the introductions, and Gabriella beamed and said, "*Enchantée.*" Then Amelia cleared the dishes, Diane got out a pen and the papers for the rental agreement, and they all sat around the kitchen table.

"We'll go month by month for now," Diane said.

"Perfect." Gabriella picked up the pen and started filling in information.

Amelia watched Gabriella write, admiring her nails, which were long, tapered and painted bright purple. Gabriella put the pen down. "There. I put both of our cell numbers, so if there's an emergency or something, you can reach one of us."

"Do you have day jobs?" Diane said.

What her mom really meant was, *Can you pay the rent each month?* Amelia crossed her fingers.

"I give pedicures and manicures in a little salon on Cassiar Street," Gabriella said.

"I work from home," Duke said. "I do consulting work."

"Really. Consulting for what?"

"Lots of things." Duke glanced at Gabriella. "Some of my clients might be coming around. I hope that's okay."

"Well, yes," Diane said slowly. "I can't see that being a problem. I have to admit, you're both much younger than I was expecting. I really should have asked you for references…you do have references, don't you?"

"Oh," Duke said. "Well, not actually *with* us, but I'm sure we could get some."

"Of course we could!" Gabriella said. "Our last landlords liked us very much!"

Diane gazed at Gabriella. "Did they? Well, I suppose it doesn't matter. No one else wants the apartment. And now, how about some iced tea? And Amelia, you could put those cookies on a plate."

"Iced tea and cookies on such a hot night," Gabriella said. "*Délicieux*!"

✵ ✵ ✵

Amelia set her alarm clock for twenty minutes to twelve. Whatever was happening at midnight, she would be ready. She brushed her teeth and popped into her mom's room to say goodnight.

Diane was in bed, reading a textbook. She was taking courses at Vancouver Career College to be a massage therapist. She said she wasn't going to work for minimum wage selling old ladies clothes at Miss Jane's forever. Lots of times, if Amelia got up for a drink in the middle of the night, she'd find her mom snoring with an open book on her lap.

"Can I get a tattoo?" Amelia said from the doorway.

"Amelia—"

"Please. Just a little one. It wouldn't—"

"No. Absolutely not. Not a chance. You're eleven years old. If I let you get a tattoo, you'll want a lip ring next."

"But—"

"No." Diane stared down at her page. "And you can't wear mascara either. Or dye your hair bright red."

"I think Gabriella's gorgeous!" Amelia said.

"Me too. She's lovely. Now I've really got to finish this chapter. Off to bed, sweetie."

Amelia paused in the doorway. "I just have one more thing to say. You don't *know* that Gabriella dyed her hair."

Behind her book, Diane snorted.

THREE

ripes. Why was her alarm ringing in the middle of the night? Amelia groped around on her night table until she felt her clock. She pushed the button down and muttered, "Shut up!" Then she remembered. Duke was meeting Simon somewhere at midnight. She bolted upright.

Footsteps crunched on gravel. Amelia scrambled out of bed and stumbled over to her open window. The only streetlight was at the end of the block, so she couldn't see much. But she could make out a shape moving down the walk to the street. Duke. A few seconds later the motorcycle roared to life, and he was gone.

He might be gone for hours. Amelia went to the kitchen and got a glass of iced tea and carried it to her bedroom. She turned on her lamp and dug in her backpack for her French conversation book, buried at the bottom under her gym shorts and three school newsletters.

She read the dialogue at the beginning of chapter one, which was mostly people saying, "*Bonjour*" and talking about the weather. That was pretty well all they'd been doing in class for two years. They still couldn't really *say* anything. Mrs. Pearson, who taught French, had to keep checking her teacher's guide, and she didn't make her *r*'s at all like Gabriella's. And where were the elegant words like *on-shon-tay*?

Amelia turned to the dictionary at the back of the book. Gabriella had said an interesting word when Duke cracked his head. It had sounded like *mare*, with maybe a *d* on the end. She scanned the row of *m* words, but she couldn't find anything that fit. A swearword, she guessed.

She flopped back against her pillow and tried counting in French to one hundred. The number seventy was hard (you had to say "sixty plus ten" or something like that) and she got all mixed up. What was she trying to prove waiting up for Duke anyway? She turned off her lamp and fell back asleep.

Duke's motorcycle jolted her awake. She leaped out of bed and sped over to the window. A single headlight, followed by a pair of headlights, advanced down the street. Duke's motorcycle pulled over in front of their house, the dark shape of Simon's van right behind it.

Amelia stayed hidden at the side of the window and watched Duke and Simon stagger back and forth between the van and the side of the house, where they disappeared. They were carrying big, bulky things that they slid out of the back of the van, each of them holding on to an end. Amelia couldn't tell what the things were, but they looked heavy.

She heard muffled exclamations from Duke. "Be careful!" "You're tipping it!" "Shhhh! Don't make so much noise." And Simon's exasperated, "Could you just relax, little bro?"

Water sloshed back and forth. Something gave a shrill squeak. A voice cried, "Beaker! Beaker! Beaker!"

Finally Simon came back by himself, slammed the rear door of the van, jumped into the driver's seat and sped away.

Amelia pulled a pair of sweatpants and a T-shirt over her pajamas and hurried out of the house, easing the front door shut behind her. She slipped around to the back. A light was shining from the apartment window beside the door, and she saw Duke and Gabriella standing in the kitchen, talking.

The two bedroom lights were on. Amelia sidled along the wall and peered into the first room. It was the small bedroom, the one that had been empty.

It wasn't empty now. It was full of cages, glass tanks and plastic bins. She stared through the side of a wire cage at a bright black eye in a grayish-green scaly face. It looked like a little dinosaur!

A hand clamped down hard on her shoulder.

Amelia spun around.

FOUR

uke! Amelia wriggled out of his grasp. Duke was big, but she wasn't going to let him freak her out. "What's going on?" she demanded.

Duke gave her a long, hard look. "Are you one of those kids who has to blab everything?"

"No! I'm awesome at keeping secrets."

"Then you'd better come inside."

Amelia followed Duke into the apartment. "Look who I found," he said to Gabriella, who was kneeling on the kitchen floor beside a huge blue plastic bin full of water.

"Amelia!" Gabriella said.

Amelia dropped down onto the floor beside Gabriella and peered into the bin. Two round turtles, the size of dinner plates, swam lazily under the water. "Wow! They're enormous!"

"Romeo and Juliet," Gabriella said. "They used to be cute and small, but they grew and now nobody wants them."

"Beaker! Beaker! Beaker!" cried a voice.

Amelia gazed around.

"Beaker! Beaker! Beaker!"

It was coming from a cage at the end of the kitchen counter. Amelia walked over to have a look. She went cold inside with shock. "Oh my god," she whispered. In the cage was a slim bird with sleek white feathers. His body looked normal. But his shoulders and neck were naked, the skin gray and scaly. He had a tiny bald head, with a few tufts of white down sticking up, and a scraggly white goatee.

"What happened to him?" Amelia said.

"Burned," Duke said. "He escaped from his cage and got under a hot tub. They're chemical burns, so he might have got into the filter or something. We don't know for sure. The person who used to own him wouldn't say. He just wanted to get rid of him."

Duke spoke quietly, but Amelia could hear anger simmering in his voice.

"We call him Beaker," Gabriella said. "Do not worry—he is not suffering. We have had him for five years now."

"So his feathers won't grow back?" Amelia said.

"Not on his head and neck," Duke said. "He didn't have any feathers at all when we got him, so he's better off now. But Beaker doesn't care anyway. He doesn't know what he looks like."

"What kind of bird is he?" Amelia said.

"A cockatiel." Gabriella sighed. "He should have lovely red cheeks and a yellow crest."

"How did you get him?"

Duke looked at Gabriella. "I guess we better tell you," Duke said. "We run a kind of shelter for abandoned and sick reptiles, and a few other strays as well. Like Beaker and"— he pointed to a cage resting on the floor by the fridge—"Zak and Lysander."

Amelia squatted beside the cage. Two fuzzy brown faces with huge round ears stared at her. "They're brothers," Duke said. "They're called Dumbo rats because of their big ears. They were cute when they were babies, and then they got big. Owner didn't want them anymore. Same old story."

"Like the turtles," Amelia said. "Do they bite?"

"Never!" Duke said. "They're both sweethearts! Zak has lung scarring, and he lets me give him medicine every day and never does a thing."

Amelia rocked back on her heels, her head spinning. "I want to see everything."

"Okay," Duke said slowly. "I'll show you the reptile room. We're setting it up in the spare bedroom. But only for a sec. I want to turn their light out. They're pretty stressed from the move, and they'll be calmer in the dark."

Duke took Amelia into the bedroom and shut the door firmly. "I'm trying to warm it up in here. These are desert and tropical animals. They can't get cold."

Two heaters glowed in corners of the room. Cages and glass tanks were lined up against the walls. "I'll be putting up some shelves," Duke said. "So I can get some of them up higher where it's warmer. But they're okay for now."

Amelia felt like eyes were peering at her from every direction. A prickle of excitement ran up her back.

"A quick tour," Duke said, "and then we'll leave them alone. You've already met Bill, I think. Through the window. He's an iguana."

Bill was draped along a thick branch, his long striped tail hanging down. A row of spikes stood up on his back, and a long flap of green skin dangled under his chin.

"He's so big," Amelia said. "He looks strong."

"Don't go too close—"

The iguana lunged at the bars and snapped his jaws.

"Yikes!" Amelia leaped back. "What's *his* problem?"

"He's a little cranky now. He thinks he's supposed to be looking for a mate."

"A *little*?" Amelia studied the iguana from a safe distance. His small dark eyes glared at her. "Does he have teeth?"

"Yeah. They're tiny, but they're sharp! But don't worry. He'll be his happy-go-lucky self again soon. You'll see— you'll be able to hold him in your arms."

Not a chance, Amelia thought.

She walked around the room slowly. She spotted a slim bright-green lizard, a fat yellow-and-black snake coiled up in a ball, a funny little creature with a grinning mouth, and a bright-red frog.

"I've never heard of a red frog," Amelia said.

"That's Nate. He's a tomato frog. They come from Madagascar. The red color keeps predators away."

Amelia peered into three tanks that looked empty except for crumpled-up towels.

"Is there anything under those towels?"

"Snakes."

Next, Amelia's eyes darted to a large wooden box that took up a corner of the room. It had low sides and was heaped full of hay. Was there anything in there? She couldn't be sure.

A pile of hay moved and a humped back poked through, then a small head on the end of a long papery neck.

"Another turtle!" Amelia said, kneeling beside the box.

"A sulcata tortoise," Duke said. "Not the same thing at all. This is Winston."

Winston took slow, lumbering steps through the hay and stopped right in front of Amelia.

"He's looking at me!" Amelia said.

The colors on his shell were beautiful. Yellows, browns and golds. "Is he old?"

"Nope. About four, I think. He could live to a hundred. And he'll get much bigger."

Amelia reached out her hand and gently touched his bumpy shell.

"We've only had him a couple of weeks. Someone found him in a drainage ditch by a farm in Langley. He'd been abandoned there."

"Is he okay?"

"Can't tell yet. We're keeping an eye on him. It was when it was really rainy and cold out. We're praying he didn't pick up some kind of respiratory disease. That can be fatal for a tortoise. And it could take a while to show up."

"Who would just leave him in a ditch?" Amelia said. "That's so horrible!"

"You wouldn't believe what some morons will do. Dogs and cats get shoved out of cars right on the freeway. Or tossed in Dumpsters."

"Why would people do that?"

"Who knows? I've heard so many horror stories. Come on. I'm going to turn the lights off now."

Amelia thought Winston was amazing. It was hard to take her eyes away from him. "Goodnight," she said softly. "And hey, please don't get sick."

Duke took Amelia to the living room to see Georgia, a soft white-and-brown lop-eared bunny (with epilepsy, Duke said), and Mary, a crested gecko (missing her tail) who peeked at her from behind a green plastic bush. Then they went back to the kitchen, where Gabriella was unpacking plastic baggies from the freezer chest. "Frozen mice," she said as she popped them into the freezer at the top of the fridge. "To feed the snakes."

"The thing is," Duke said, "we weren't going to tell your mom about the animals. Not just yet."

"We do not want to lie to her," Gabriella said quickly. "We will tell her soon. So many landlords have told us no animals. If we wait one or two weeks and then tell your mother, she will know that they will not hurt anybody, and she will let us stay."

"That's the plan," Duke said.

"So you will keep our secret?" Gabriella added.

"Of course I will! But there's one problem. A *mega* problem. Mom has this snake phobia."

"We'll phase her in slowly," Duke said. "Introduce them one at a time—"

"I'm talking a *serious* snake phobia," Amelia said.

Duke was silent for a moment.

"Like, how serious?"

"Like, try going ballistic if she even sees a picture of one."

FIVE

The next morning, Amelia's eyes felt like they had sand in them. She'd been way too hyper to sleep when she had finally got back to bed. Excited and worried at the same time. Duke didn't know her mother.

She walked along their street, past houses of all different sizes and colors. Most of their neighbors had at least some garden area, and their grass was mowed. Diane had run over a rock and broken their lawn mower, so their lawn looked like a hayfield. It was embarrassing.

Maybe that was why their neighbors ignored them. Or maybe it was just that kind of neighborhood. Diane said most of the people here worked all day and were busy. Maybe, thought Amelia.

She and her mom had been living here for almost a year, and they didn't know *one* person. Not even the woman next door, who was always weeding her garden but who hadn't even looked up a week ago when Amelia said hello. A couple from India lived on the other side, and she saw them sometimes, getting into their silver car. The man wore jeans, but the woman always dressed in a colorful sari. The Indian couple's house was the last one on their street, which dead-ended at a chain-link fence behind a high school.

In their old neighborhood, the houses were nicer. Most of the families had lived there a long time, and they all knew Amelia. Her best friend, Starla, had been only three doors away, and they had practically lived at each other's houses.

Halfway down the street, Amelia stopped to admire the red sports car that had appeared a few weeks ago in the driveway of a small green house. She had never seen a car that was so bright and shiny, like a mirror, with so much glittering chrome. She had told her friend Liam last week that it was probably a Ferrari, and he had said, *Do you have any idea how much Ferraris cost?* Then he'd raced over after school to check it out.

Get your cars straight, Amelia, he'd said. *It's a Mustang.*

But he was impressed, Amelia could tell, and they had both walked around it and peered in the windows. Then the front door of the house had burst open, and a skinny guy in jeans with holes in the knees and a stud in his lip had yelled at them, *Get away! Don't put your fingerprints on it! Don't even breathe on it!*

Amelia had fled to the safety of the street, but Liam had sauntered away, yelling over his shoulder, *Okay, okay, dude. Yeesh!*

GET LOST, PUNK! the guy hollered, and Liam had stopped sauntering and broken into a jog.

Nice neighborhood, he'd muttered.

This morning, Amelia spotted a bucket by the back door of the car. It looked like the bucket was full of polishing rags, and she started to run in case the skinny guy came out and screamed again. She ran the two blocks to Hastings Street, crossed at a light and walked three more blocks to her school. She found her friends, Roshni and Liam, sitting in the sun with their backs against the outside gym wall. Roshni was reading a *People* magazine. Liam had earbuds jammed in his ears, and his eyes were closed.

"*Bonjour!*" Amelia dumped her backpack on the ground and slid down the wall beside them.

"*Bon voyage*," Roshni said, flipping pages without looking up.

Liam yanked out his earbuds. "What?"

"We're speaking French," Roshni said.

"We rented the apartment!" Amelia burst out.

Roshni closed her magazine. "You're kidding! Who to?"

"Gabriella and Duke. Gabriella's from Paris! She's a real French person!"

"How can you be a fake French person?" Liam said.

Amelia ignored him. "They are very cool. *Very* cool. They moved in yesterday." A wide smile spread across her face.

"Gah!" Liam leaped up as if he were going to run away. "When are you going to do something about that tooth? You are seriously scary!"

"Shut up, Liam," Roshni said. "And sit down. What's so cool about them?"

Amelia opened her mouth. She was about to say, *They have a SNAKE! Wait, not one snake! Lots of snakes! And an iguana and a tortoise and rats and this bird—*

But she clamped her mouth shut. She'd promised Duke she could keep a secret. Did he mean from just her mom, or did he mean from everybody?

"Well?" Roshni demanded.

"They're just really neat," Amelia said. *Whoops.* Big mistake bringing this up, especially with someone like Roshni. "Gabriella's French."

Roshni's eyes narrowed. "You already said that. And you hate French."

"I don't *hate* French. I just hate the way Mrs. Pearson teaches it."

"Right." Roshni dug in her backpack and pulled out a well-worn *Star* magazine.

Time to change the subject fast. "Is that a new iPod?" Amelia said to Liam.

Liam pulled out his earbuds again. "What?"

"A new iPod?"

"Yeah."

"What was wrong with the old one?"

Liam shrugged. "This one can do more stuff. Dad got it for me."

Liam's parents were divorced, which was a lot more final than the situation with Amelia's parents, who were separated. Liam's dad was rich and bought him stuff all the time.

"Oh, wow," Roshni said. "Lindsay Lohan is back in jail."

"Who cares?" Amelia said. "Don't you think you're getting a little bit too obsessed with celebrities?"

"Pardon me? I'm obsessed? *I'm* obsessed? This coming from you, who only talks about Camp Fly Away, like, all day long?"

"Camp Soar Like an Eagle." That was unfair. She didn't talk about it that much. She'd found the camp on the Internet. It was about three hundred miles away from Vancouver, somewhere in the Cariboo. There was a climbing wall and a sweat lodge, and they took you mountain climbing. She checked every day, and there were still a few openings.

"Speaking of Camp Whatever," Liam said, "what did your dad say?"

"He said no. It's mega expensive."

The bell rang, and Roshni shoved her magazines into her backpack. "I say you're hiding something about those people who took your apartment," she said unexpectedly. "Nice, Amelia."

Amelia felt her cheeks turn red. "I'm not."

She and Starla had never argued as much as she and Roshni did. She missed Starla, but whenever they tried to get together it ended up being so complicated, organizing rides and working around all the stuff they had to do, that it never happened. She sighed. It was hot already. She should have worn a tank top instead of this stupid sweatshirt. She felt as prickly as a hedgehog.

✼ ✼ ✼

When Amelia got home from school, Diane was in her bedroom, on the phone. It was Friday, Diane's day off because she worked on Saturdays. Amelia poured herself a glass of milk. She could hear her mom yelling from all the way down the hall.

"I don't *care* if the twins want to join hockey and the roof needs new shingles! I'd appreciate some child support!"

Amelia winced.

"It's called postpartum depression. Deal with it!"

Silence.

Amelia sighed. Dad sounded broke. No way he was going to change his mind and fork out the money for Camp Soar Like an Eagle.

"Oh, sweetie!" Diane said from the doorway. "I didn't know you were home. I hope you didn't hear all that."

Diane had read a book about kids and divorce when she and Amelia's dad split up. She'd promised Amelia she would never bad-mouth her father to her or make her a pawn in their fights, even if worse came to worst and they ended up getting a divorce. (Amelia didn't want to even go there.) Most of the time, Diane had stuck to it.

"That's okay." Amelia pointed to a brand-new blender sitting on the counter. "Where'd that come from?"

"An amazing sale at London Drugs. Half price!"

Diane was into making green smoothies full of healthy things like broccoli and spinach. The new blender looked great. Very high-tech.

"I thought I'd give the old one to Gabriella. I know it only has one speed that works, but she might be able to use it. I wonder if they're married," Diane added as she lifted the old blender down from the cupboard above the fridge.

"What?"

"I wonder if they're married."

"Why does it matter?"

"It doesn't matter. And I'm not criticizing them. I'm just wondering."

"You sound like you're *going* to criticize them. People live together these days, Mom. They don't have to get married."

"I'm well aware of *that*, Amelia."

Her dad and Candice. How could she be so dumb? "Sorry," Amelia mumbled.

"Nothing to be sorry about. I'll pop down with this now. I saw Gabriella come in just after lunch."

"No!" Amelia said. "I'll take it!"

"I want to look at the apartment. Make sure everything's okay."

"You can't. I mean, it's fine! Everything's fine. I'm going to see Gabriella anyway. There's something I want to ask her in my French homework—"

"You're babbling, Amelia Jane."

Amelia sealed her lips.

"Okay. You go," her mother said. "But tell her if she doesn't want the blender my feelings won't be hurt. It can go to the thrift store."

"Right." Amelia fled with the blender. Keeping this secret was turning out to be a nightmare.

SIX

The apartment door was propped open with a sandal. Amelia stuck her head in. Gabriella was sitting at the small kitchen table, clipping something with a pair of scissors. Little pieces of paper were scattered across the table, and more papers were crammed into a shoe box.

Gabriella's red hair was tied in a messy bun on top of her head, and her eyes were rimmed with black. "*Salut*, Amelia. *Entrez.*"

"I wasn't sure you'd be here," Amelia said. "I thought you had to work at the salon today."

"Me too. But there were no clients booked for this afternoon, so they sent me home. That happened last week too."

Amelia walked over to the table. The pieces of paper turned out to be store coupons. Gabriella had hundreds of them.

"That's a ton of coupons," Amelia said. "What are you doing?"

"Sorting." Gabriella picked up a small stack and stuck it in the shoe box, behind a piece of cardboard sticking up that said *Cleaning*.

"What are you going to do with them all?"

"Save money! Doesn't your mother coupon?"

"No. She's too tired when we get to the store. Or in a rush. But she usually looks for sales in the flyers."

"There was a woman on TV who coupons," Gabriella said. "She saved $30,000 in one year."

"Wow!"

"She is…what do you call it…an extreme couponer. She has inspired me. I want to be an extreme couponer too. Duke and I are always needing more money. And now things are dead at the salon. I really can not afford to have afternoons off." She cut out a coupon for Crest toothpaste and slid it into the shoe box behind *Bathroom*.

Amelia picked up one of the coupons and read out loud, "*Save 75 cents on BIG G CEREALS when you buy ONE BOX of Honey Nut Cheerios*. That's a good deal."

"Of course. Duke adores Cheerios. We will file that under *Breakfast*."

"Where do you get them all?"

"I pick them up at stores. In newspapers. Mostly off the Internet—dealcatcher.com and savealoonie.com. Here is a good one—two dollars off any Revlon beauty tool." She tucked it into the shoe box behind *Gabriella*.

Amelia read some of the other categories out loud. *Animals, Health, Entertainment, Clothes*.

"Sometimes it is hard to know where to put it." Gabriella picked up a coupon. "*As seen on TV. Ab Rocket Twister. With DVD workouts. $129.99.* That could go in *Health* or *Entertainment.* Or *Gabriella.* Duke would never use it."

Amelia watched Gabriella clip and sort. Three more coupons for toothpaste. "You're going to have a lot of toothpaste," she said.

She wandered over to Beaker's cage. She felt sick when she saw his scrawny neck and bald head. "Hey, Beaker, how are you doing? You're awfully quiet today."

"He will be noisy again at night when it starts to get dark."

"Where's Duke?"

"He has gone to pick up some ferrets. Some kids found them in a box in an alley. I am thinking they will be very hungry. And maybe sick. But Duke will know what to do."

Amelia wasn't exactly sure what a ferret was. But it sounded interesting.

The bin with the turtles had been moved into the hallway. Amelia remembered their names. Romeo and Juliet. They were nibbling on little brown pellets floating on the surface of the water. One of the turtles clambered onto a plastic platform that bobbed up and down. Did it feel the same as floating on an air mattress, like she had done last summer for hours and hours when they rented a cabin at Cultus Lake for a week?

That was what she remembered about that week— lying on the air mattress, even though it was cool and rainy most days, thinking about how much she hated Dad.

Mom had been mostly on her cell phone—setting up an appointment with a lawyer and making arrangements to have Great-Aunt Mildred's house cleaned so they could move in.

Amelia sighed. Why was she thinking about that now?

She slipped into the reptile room. It was hot, like a sauna. A small red light glowed on each of the heaters. Round lightbulbs, shining brightly, hung from the sides of some of the cages.

Amelia went right to Winston's pen. "Hey, Winston," she said.

The tortoise was chewing on a wispy piece of hay. He didn't look sick. But how could you tell with a tortoise? She wanted to touch his wrinkly neck, just to see what it felt like, but he might not like that.

Winston's jaws moved up and down slowly. His black eyes blinked at Amelia.

What was he thinking about? He'd been dumped in a cold, wet drainage ditch. Did he worry about that? Was he paranoid that someone would abandon him again?

"You must have freaked out," Amelia said. "But don't worry. Duke and Gabriella will look after you. I promise."

Duke had said that the animals were desert and tropical animals. She didn't know which one Winston was. He was a special kind of tortoise—Duke had told her the name, but she couldn't remember it.

She stood up. "I'm just going to say hi to everyone else. I'll be back in a minute."

The iguana, Bill, looked like he was asleep, but Amelia stayed well back just in case. The yellow-and-black snake was still curled up in a ball, each coil as thick as her arm. She peered into the tanks with the towels. One snake, skinny with black and white stripes like a zebra, had slithered out, but the other two snakes were still hidden.

She felt like someone was watching her and glanced up at the brown creature with the grinning mouth. "Who are you?" she said, smiling.

Amelia opened the door of the reptile room. "What's that little brown guy called?"

"Apollo," Gabriella said. "He is a bearded dragon. And the green lizard is Kilo. She is a Chinese water dragon."

Dragons! Such big names for such little creatures.

"The ferrets are here!" Gabriella said.

✢ ✢ ✢

There were three ferrets. Duke said they were related to weasels and let Amelia reach into the box and pick them up, one at a time. They were long and skinny, with thick fur. One was almost all white, with a dusting of black, and the other two were brown and white with black around their eyes.

"A group of ferrets is called a business," Duke said. "You know, like a herd of cows? Well, it's a business of ferrets. So I thought we'd call these guys The Secretary, The Accountant and The President."

Amelia grinned. She held up the white ferret by its middle. Its head and tail dangled down. "Which one is this?"

"The Accountant," Duke said.

"He's so bendy," Amelia said.

"Their spines have to be flexible so they can wiggle into holes in the ground."

"Are they okay?"

"I think so. Maybe a little skinny, and I'm going to check for eye infections."

Amelia helped Duke set up the ferrets' cage in the living room, next to Georgia the rabbit and the crested gecko Mary. They strung a blue hammock from one side of the cage to the other. The ferrets clambered into the hammock and settled in a furry heap.

"They'll sleep now," Duke said. "Ferrets spend most of their lives sleeping. About twenty hours a day. I'm not kidding. And now I've got something to show you. Have you ever held a snake before?"

"No," Amelia said.

"Come with me."

Amelia followed Duke into the reptile room. He reached into a tank and lifted up the black-and-white-striped snake.

He handed him to Amelia. "This is a California king-snake. His name is Zebra."

Zebra was squirmy, slithering partway up her arm. But he wasn't slimy. His skin felt dry and cool.

"Look at his eyes," Duke said. "What do they look like to you?"

"Kind of bluish?"

"They turned that way this morning. It means he's getting ready to shed. His eyes will go clear again in a few days, and then he'll get rid of his skin."

"Is he sick or something?"

"Nope. All snakes shed their skins. It's because they're growing, and their skin doesn't stretch like a human's."

"I'd love to see him do that."

"I'll come and get you. If you're not at school."

"Thanks!"

Duke and Gabriella were the best thing that had happened since Amelia and her mom had moved here. But how was she supposed to keep all of this a secret? A rat, ferrets, lizards, *snakes*. If her mom found out, she'd freak. She'd never let Gabriella and Duke stay.

Never.

SEVEN

"**T**his is interesting," Liam said.

He was sitting cross-legged on the grass in Roshni's backyard, surrounded by a sea of newspaper. Roshni and Amelia lay on towels in their bikinis. They were supposed to be working on their tans, but Roshni's skin was brown anyway, and Amelia thought it was unfair to compare her tan to Roshni's.

Roshni had parked herself for the day. She had a stack of *Star* and *People* magazines, a water bottle and a bag of chocolate-chip cookies. Amelia tried to sneak peeks at her watch. The backs of her knees were burning, and she really wanted to go home.

Zebra was probably shedding his skin right now, and she was missing it. His eyes had turned blue on Friday, and today was Sunday. And Duke had said she could help clean cages today. She'd only come over to Roshni's because she couldn't think of an excuse fast enough when Roshni phoned her that morning. Roshni was bossy, and Amelia had been half asleep. She'd promised herself she'd just stay for a little while.

Liam had showed up on his bike half an hour ago, with today's *Vancouver Sun* under his rat trap. Great. She had only two friends, and one of them read junk celebrity magazines, while the other read newspapers. She was the only normal one. She rolled over on her back and watched a puffy white cloud drift across the blue sky.

"Very interesting," Liam repeated from behind the newspaper.

"Okay, what is it?" Amelia propped herself up on her elbow. There was no point hoping Liam would go away. He could be as persistent as a mosquito.

"This is an article about lying," Liam said. "Famous liars in history, like ex-president Clinton, and how to tell if someone is lying and stuff like that. Here's a picture of Lance Armstrong. The slime."

"Who's Lance Armstrong?" Roshni said from the depths of her magazine.

"Roshni," Liam said, "where have you been? Do you live under a rock or something? You really need to watch the news once in a while. And I don't mean *Entertainment Tonight*. Lance Armstrong won the Tour de France seven times, and he's admitted he used drugs. He's been lying about it forever."

"Oh," Roshni said.

"*On average, people tell at least two lies a day, every day of their lives,*" Liam read.

"I don't," Roshni said.

"Ha! That's probably a lie right there!" Liam kept reading. "*Daily life deception, on the little-white-lies scale, is necessary for good social relationships. Imagine a world where everyone told the truth. It would soon spiral into chaos—*"

Roshni groaned.

"Do you want to hear the rest?" Liam said a bit huffily.

"Keep going," Amelia said. Was keeping a secret the same as lying? "Read the part about how you tell if someone is lying."

"Okay. *Liars stare too long and too hard. They blink twice as frequently as truth-tellers. They are more likely to raise their eyebrows. They smirk when they're trying to look sad. They use increased speech hesitations like ums and ers—*"

"We get the picture." Roshni pulled her bikini strap down on her shoulder to check her tan. "Amelia, will you come with me to the Lougheed Mall after school tomorrow? I'm allowed to get some new jeans."

"Tomorrow?" Amelia had already missed most of the day with the animals.

She almost blurted out her secret, but then she changed her mind. Liam wouldn't give it away, but Roshni would probably spill the beans accidentally to Amelia's mom. That's what Roshni was like.

Roshni was staring at her.

"I'm going to the dentist tomorrow," Amelia said.

A lie. It just popped out.

"I thought you said your appointment was on Tuesday."

"I have two appointments." Second lie. She'd also lied to her mom that morning. When Diane said she was going to go downstairs to ask Duke if he knew anything about fixing lawn mowers, Amelia had told her Duke had a headache and was resting. So she was up to three lies already. Above the average. What kind of person did that make her?

Amelia displayed her jagged tooth to Roshni. "It's going to take at least two appointments to fix." She paused. "Maybe more."

She tried not to blink, and she forced her eyebrows to behave themselves. Had she said um or er? She wasn't sure. Her cheeks felt on fire.

Roshni turned back to her magazine. "If you say so."

"Roshni's mad at me," Amelia said, kneeling beside Winston's pen. "And I really miss Starla." Tears pushed against the backs of her eyes, and her nose stuffed up. It caught her off guard. She usually tried hard not to think about her old best friend. At least, she had since their last phone call, when Starla had only talked for two minutes and then said she was going to a movie with Amber. *Amber*, who had been their sworn enemy all through grades four and five.

Amelia swiped at her eyes. "Roshni ignored me all day. It sucks." She sighed. "Let's change the subject. Do you know you're a sulcata tortoise? I asked Duke. I googled it last night. It's pretty neat, really."

Winston waded through the hay, heading toward a shallow bowl of water. Amelia loved watching his stubby legs move in and out of his shell.

"You come from the edge of the Sahara Desert. Well, not you, but maybe your mother or your grandmother. You came from a pet store, I guess."

Amelia didn't want to make Winston feel sad. "But hey, deserts aren't all that great. There are lots of prickly cactuses. And Duke said that if it's hot again tomorrow and not too breezy, I can take you outside on the grass for a while."

Winston opened and closed his eyes.

Amelia remembered something else the article she'd found online had said. *Sulcata tortoises cannot be allowed to get chilled and wet.*

There'd been a lot about respiratory illness. It sounded really bad. Did Winston look the same as yesterday? What was she supposed to even look for? Amelia got up carefully. She'd scorched the back of her knees at Roshni's yesterday, and it hurt to move quickly. She'd ask Duke.

Duke was lying on the couch in the living room with a laptop on his stomach, talking on his phone. "Yeah, we're getting low. Just some mice left…Okay, ten fuzzies, ten pups, a dozen hoppers and fifteen jumbos…Next week. Great."

"What's that all about?" Amelia said.

"An order for frozen rats. They come in different sizes."

Was Duke kidding? "*Fuzzies?*"

"They're the smallest. Like your pinkie. They're just babies."

"For the snakes, right?"

"Right."

Amelia sighed. Was she really feeling sorry for dead rats? It was a bit confusing when just last night Zak had been sitting on her shoulder, nibbling her ear.

"Do you think Winston's okay?"

"He's fine."

"Are you sure?"

"Sure. I just checked him a little while ago."

Amelia lowered herself into a saggy armchair. Duke passed her his laptop so she could see the photos he was uploading to his website. She thought the name of the website, Duke's Den, was perfect. There was a great photo of the ferrets piled in their hammock, one of the bearded dragon, Apollo, grinning at the camera and one of Bill scowling through the bars of his cage.

She heard the shower in the bathroom shut off. A few minutes later Gabriella came out, wearing shorts and a tank top, her hair wrapped in a white towel. "Hey, Amelia. I have Rocky Road ice cream. Two-for-one coupon. You can get everybody some while I comb my hair."

Amelia chatted to Beaker while she got out three bowls and spoons. The carton of ice cream was near the front of the freezer, surrounded by the baggies of frozen mice.

She carried the bowls into the living room. Duke balanced his bowl in front of his laptop and took bites while he typed.

Amelia could hear Gabriella in the bedroom, talking to someone on her phone. She was taking a long time. Her bowl of ice cream was melting into a puddle, and Amelia was wondering if she should stick it in the fridge when Gabriella came into the living room.

"That was the salon! They are cutting me back. They only want me three days a week."

"What?" Duke stopped typing. "Crap! They can't do that!"

"They just did." Gabriella pushed Duke's feet off the end of the couch and sank down. "Now what are we going to do?"

She buried her face in her hands. "*Merde!*"

She looked up. "Oops. That is not a good word for you to hear, Amelia. Promise me you won't say it."

"I promise."

Amelia took the ice-cream bowls into the kitchen and poured Gabriella's soupy ice cream down the sink.

"Beaker. Beaker. Beaker," Beaker said softly.

"I'm going now," Amelia called out, but no one answered her. She let herself out the door. She could hear Duke and Gabriella fighting about what vet bill they should pay first. Gabriella was crying.

EIGHT

"*Merde!*" Amelia pulled her pillow over her head. Today was her dentist appointment.

Two years ago, Amelia had gone in to have a cavity filled, and something went wrong with the freezing, only no one knew that until the drill hit a nerve. Amelia had screamed. Her mom, who was in the waiting room, had been furious. They had changed dentists, and Diane had promised it would never happen again.

But Amelia's stomach still turned in somersaults on dentist days. She stumbled to the kitchen, where Diane was watching something pale green swirl in the new blender.

"I'm going to guzzle this and run." Diane poured the green mess into a glass. "Make sure you eat some breakfast. I've left bus money on the table by the door. There's enough so you can go to Dairy Queen after, if you want."

Amelia brightened. "I don't have to go to school?"

"Your reward for going to the dentist without making a fuss. Besides, I have an ulterior motive. I'd like someone to be here this afternoon. One of the women in my class is giving me a massage table she doesn't want anymore. Her husband, Frank, is going to drop it off, and I'd rather it wasn't left outside." Diane hesitated. "You won't miss any important tests, will you?"

A *quiz* on capital cities wasn't exactly a *test*. So it wasn't exactly a lie. "Don't worry. I won't miss anything," Amelia said.

The dentist appointment was a breeze. When Dr. Phillips finished, she made Amelia smile into a mirror. "Now you look like a human being again. We'll put a permanent crown on when you're older. This will do you for a few years."

Amelia headed straight to DQ. Her strawberry milkshake was hard to drink because of the freezing in her mouth. She moved the straw to the good side of her mouth and checked her watch. She was missing social studies and library and…science. She'd forgotten about science. The class was making posters on global warming. She was Roshni's partner, and the posters absolutely had to be finished today. Mr. Howard was going to give a prize (movie tickets, the rumor was!) for the best one.

One more reason for Roshni to want to kill her.

✵ ✵ ✵

"Do you think Duke is selling drugs?" Diane said.

She was standing at the kitchen window, watching the street and dipping a spoon into a tub of yogurt.

"Mom!"

"He was very evasive when he talked about his clients. And some guy on a motorcycle was just here. I thought he was wearing a flowered shirt, and then I realized it was tattoos. His arms were covered in them! They left together a few minutes ago."

"That doesn't mean anything," Amelia said. "And why aren't you at Miss Jane's?"

"I decided to come home for lunch. Less temptation. Now smile for me. Let me see."

Amelia smiled.

"Perfect! How was it?"

"Fine."

Amelia was disappointed that Duke had gone out. She'd planned to leave a note on the door for the man with the massage table and then hang out at the apartment.

"I don't know what time I'll be back," Diane said. "Late for sure. I'm helping Miss Jane with the inventory. And then, hallelujah, I can sleep in for a whole month!"

Diane's holidays started the next day. It was a slow time at the clothing store, and Diane always said how much she liked being home with Amelia for at least part of the summer. She tossed the empty yogurt tub into the recycling bin. "I'll call that woman who rented us the cabin at Cultus last year. It's probably taken, but she might know someone else who has a cabin."

"Let's just stay home." Amelia's memories of Cultus Lake weren't great.

"You're sure?"

"Yup."

"Okay then, I'm off. Remember, Frank's coming with the table."

Amelia waited until her mother was safely gone before she turned on the laptop. She was supposed to use it only for homework. One of the advantages of being home alone. She brought up the website for Camp Soar Like an Eagle and clicked on the link for registration. There were still places available for August, but the price made her heart sink. It hadn't changed—$1,500 for two weeks.

One of Gabriella's coupons would be perfect. *Camp Soar Like an Eagle. Two weeks for the price of one.* She turned the laptop off and flipped on the TV.

The massage-table man arrived in the middle of the afternoon. When the doorbell rang, Amelia peered sideways through the living-room window. Diane always went on and on about Amelia not opening the door until she knew who it was. She could see the front step and a man standing there with something that looked like it could be a fold-up table.

Frank carried the table into the laundry room, where there was just enough room to set it up beside the washer and dryer. He showed her how to snap on the piece for people's heads, which looked like a doughnut. He was very chatty. "My wife, Jeannie, has really enjoyed meeting your mom.

She's always telling me what a riot Diane is. How she gets the whole class screaming with laughter."

Mom? Amelia looked at him in disbelief. Then she studied the table, which looked awfully rickety. Diane planned to practise on her. "Is this thing safe?"

Frank laughed. "A jokester. Just like your mom."

Frank left, and Amelia went back to the TV. Three minutes later the doorbell rang again. "Now what does he want?" she muttered. She peered through the living-room window.

It wasn't Frank. It was a girl with pink spiky hair and a lot of piercings.

Her arms were full of something brown and orange. Something that was moving as slow as syrup, twisting and coiling around the girl's neck and shoulders.

Amelia's mouth fell open.

A snake!

NINE

The girl shouted something at Amelia through the window. Amelia thought she might have said, "Where's Duke?" She decided it was safe to open the door.

"I'm looking for Duke," the girl said.

"He lives downstairs. But he's not home right now."

Amelia couldn't take her eyes off the snake. It was at least six feet long and all different shades of brown and orange swirled together. It never stopped moving, slowly slithering around the girl.

"I was supposed to be here hours ago," the girl said. "Duke probably thought I wasn't coming. My car conked out on me, and I had to walk miles because the stupid bus driver wouldn't let me on the bus. I got a lot of weird looks, I can tell you!"

"You can come in here and wait for Duke."

"I guess so. But I don't have a lot of time. I'm Pia, by the way."

"Amelia."

Pia's hands were constantly moving, keeping up with the snake. "This is King Kong. He's not exactly light. But it was easier to carry him this way than in a box."

"Is he trying to get away?"

"No. He's just a bit stressed."

Pia followed Amelia into the house. "We'll go in the kitchen," Amelia said. "Do you want a glass of water or something? Or I could make some iced tea."

"Water's good. I'm parched." Pia peeled the snake off her shoulders. "Okay if I put him on the table?"

"Sure." Amelia set a glass of water in front of Pia. She did a quick inventory of Pia's piercings. Six earrings in each ear, a nose stud, and two silver spikes in her lower lip.

King Kong took up most of the table. He curled up like a coil of thick rope and rested his head.

"Will he stay there?" Amelia said.

"I think so. He's getting tired."

Pia looked at her watch and groaned. "It's quarter after four! You don't happen to know when Duke's coming back, do you?"

"No. Sorry. Is King Kong sick or something?"

Pia looked surprised. "King Kong? No way. Duke's just going to look after him for the summer. I'm going up the coast to a fly-in fishing camp tomorrow. I go there every year and cook. And get this—they think King Kong would freak out their clients, so I can't bring him. That's so lame."

"Yeah," Amelia agreed. "What kind of snake is he?"

"Carpet python."

"He's amazing."

"You got that right." Pia drummed her fingers on the table. "How's old Beaker doing?"

"Good."

Pia whipped a phone out of her pocket. Her fingers flew as she texted. "Okay, okay," she muttered. "I'm coming."

She stuck her phone back in her pocket, drained her glass of water and looked at her watch again. "God, I've got a million things to do today. I'm gonna have to go."

"Right now?"

"'Fraid so. You'll have to watch King Kong for me until Duke gets back."

"Me? By myself?"

"That's okay, isn't it?"

"No! It's *not* okay. What if he wants to get up? It's not like he's asleep. His eyes are still open."

"Snakes don't have eyelids, so it's kind of hard to tell. He might be asleep." Pia yanked her phone out again and texted madly. She stood up. "Trust me, he's wiped. He'll crash for hours. Honestly, I *have* to go. I haven't even packed yet, and I'm leaving at, like, four in the morning. I haven't even cleaned out my fridge!"

"No."

"Pleeease."

Amelia sighed. Gabriella was always home by five, which was only a half hour away. She'd know what to do with King Kong. "Oh, all right."

Pia's face lit up. "You're a lifesaver! I owe you one!" She patted the snake's head. "See you, King Kong. Be good."

She hesitated. "Maybe you should stay beside him. Just in case. I'll let myself out. And tell Duke I'll call him."

When the front door clicked shut, Amelia's heart started to race. King Kong with Pia was not too scary. King Kong by himself was a different story. She eyeballed the snake. He wasn't moving. Not at all. Asleep or…a prickle ran down her spine. *Dead.* It was a boiling-hot day. He could have died of heatstroke.

Great. She was babysitting a dead snake. She stood up and pushed her chair back, which made a scraping sound on the floor. She sat down immediately. If King Kong was asleep and not dead after all, the last thing she wanted to do was wake him up. Did snakes have ears? How was she supposed to know?

The clock on the kitchen wall made a ticking sound as the minutes clicked by. Amelia felt like a prisoner. From her chair, she could see out the window to the front walk. She kept her eyes peeled for Gabriella. She thought about dashing into the living room and getting the laptop. It would take her fifteen seconds, max. She weighed the pros and cons.

Too risky. Snakes probably did have ears, hidden somewhere under their scales. King Kong asleep (or dead) was okay. King Kong slithering around the kitchen would be a nightmare.

She stopped thinking about the laptop and thought about how she needed to pee.

Five minutes later, still no Gabriella.

She held her breath and slid off her chair. No sign of life from King Kong. She tiptoed across the floor and, with one last glance at the snake, slipped through the door and ran.

Forty seconds in the bathroom. World record. She dried her hands on her shorts as she raced back.

She slammed right into Diane.

Diane dropped a handful of mail. "Really, Amelia. Slow down."

"Mom! What are you doing here? You're not supposed to be home for ages."

"Miss Jane had a migraine." Diane bent down to pick up the scattered letters. "We're going to go in early tomorrow to finish the inventory. And yes, it's nice to see you too." She dropped the letters on the table. "I'm going to put the kettle on and make some tea, and then I'm going to have a nice cool shower."

"No! I mean, have your shower first!"

"Amelia Jane, you are acting very strange."

"Wait! Come back! DON'T GO IN THE KITCHEN!"

Too late! Amelia clamped her hands over her ears. Even through her closed fingers, her mother's bloodcurdling scream sent chills down her spine.

TEN

"It's okay, Mom. Trust me. You're gonna be okay."

Somehow Amelia had gotten her mother out of the kitchen and onto the living-room couch. Diane was hunched over, hugging herself. She'd been crying for fifteen minutes, which was awful, and now she wasn't doing anything, which was worse.

"It's okay, Mom," Amelia repeated. "Look, I'm gonna get you some water."

Diane lifted her head. "Did you know that snake was in there?"

"Um…"

"You could have warned me!"

"I tried! I'll get the water."

Amelia hurried to the kitchen, her heart hammering. She'd left King Kong on his own for an awfully long time. Her eyes went straight to the table. Empty.

"Omigod," she moaned.

She pulled the chairs back and stuck her head under the table, peered in the space between the fridge and the stove, and cautiously opened the oven door. She knew from somewhere that snakes liked warm places, but the oven was cold unless it was being used. And how would he get in the oven anyway when the door was closed? "STOP IT!" she said. "*Think.*"

Water. She poured a glass and carried it to the living room.

"He's gone, Mom."

"Gone? Gone *where*?"

"That's the problem. I don't know."

"I don't believe this," Diane snarled. "There's a…*snake*, crawling somewhere inside my house?"

"I don't think snakes crawl. They slith—never mind. And he might just have gone somewhere to sleep. He was very tired."

"If that's supposed to make me feel better, it's not working." Diane staggered to her feet. "I'm getting out of here. And I'm not coming back inside until you find it. Is that clear?"

"Crystal."

This was one of the few times when Amelia was glad that Great-Aunt Mildred's house was tiny. She'd already eliminated the kitchen, and King Kong couldn't be in the living room or they'd have seen him. She kept her eyes peeled as she headed down the narrow hall. She searched the laundry room first, counting to ten and then pulling all the dirty clothes out of the hamper. Nothing. *Phew!* Then she peeked behind the washer and dryer.

Bathroom next. Sink—empty. Nothing lurking behind the stack of towels on the counter. She eyed the pink shower curtain pulled across the tub. She held her breath and yanked it back. No King Kong.

Her bedroom had tons of potential hiding places, including her closet (the door was open a snake-sized crack), the crumpled blankets on her unmade bed and the heaps of clothes scattered on the floor. As she searched, she became more and more frantic. She sank back on her heels after checking out the floor under her bed and brushed a dust bunny from her face. Where *was* he?

The phone ringing in Diane's room sent her flying across the hall.

"Hello…Oh, hi, Roshni."

"Where were you?" Roshni demanded.

"What?" Amelia's eyes scanned the room. Her mom was a neat freak, which helped. No snakelike bulges sticking up in the smooth, flat bedspread…closet door shut…

"I had to finish our poster all by myself, and it looked crappy because I was in such a rush, so goodbye prize!"

Amelia flipped back the curtains. She could see her mom standing in the middle of the front yard.

"Are you even listening to me?"

"No. I mean, yes. I can't talk now. I'll tell you everything later."

"That poster was *important* to me. Free movie tickets, Amelia!"

"I gotta go."

"*Fine.*"

"Like I really need this right now," Amelia muttered. She opened the window and yelled, "Did you leave the front door open when you got home from work?"

"What?" Diane called back. "No, I don't think so—wait a minute, maybe I did! I think I wanted to get some air in the house."

"Then he must be outside somewhere. I'll be right out!"

By the time Amelia got outside, Diane had moved to the other side of the street, squeezed between a parked red mini and a van. "You have a lot of explaining to do, Amelia Jane," she shouted.

Amelia stared hard at the van. She was positive she'd seen a flash of orange.

"Mom! DON'T MOVE!"

She raced across the street, got down on her hands and knees and peered between the tires. "There you are!" she cried.

She lay flat on her stomach and wiggled partway under the van. She filled her arms with thick, rubbery coils of snake and carefully inched her way back out. "Easy boy, easy boy," she murmured.

"*Mon dieu!*" said Gabriella's voice. "That is King Kong!"

Amelia looked up. Gabriella was crossing the street, her high-heeled sandals clacking on the pavement.

Diane stared at Gabriella. "You *know* this snake?"

"He's gentle, Mom. He wouldn't hurt—"

"STAY BACK!" Diane said. "Don't take ONE STEP closer! Okay, you two. I want to know what's going on. NOW!"

ELEVEN

Diane and Amelia waited outside the apartment door while Gabriella disappeared inside with King Kong. When she came back, she flashed her megawatt smile, which faded quickly when she saw Diane's tight lips, and said, "There. King Kong is locked in the bathroom. He cannot escape. And now, please come in."

Gabriella rushed Diane through the kitchen ("Excuse the dirty dishes," she apologized. "Did not hear the alarm this morning"), past the plastic bin of turtles and into the living room.

"Why are there ribbons hanging from all the doorways?" Diane said.

"Duke keeps hitting his head. The ribbons remind him to duck. But we are not complaining," Gabriella added hastily. "It is Duke's fault that he is so tall, not yours. And now, please sit down."

"I can see everything standing, thank you very much."

The living room wasn't too scary, Amelia thought. Zak and Lysander, peering through the wire mesh of their cage, weren't at all how one imagined rats would look. The ferrets were asleep in their hammock, Mary was hiding behind her plastic bush, and Georgia was Georgia—fluffy and adorable.

"Duke and Gabriella rescue animals, Mom. Mostly reptiles. Duke says you wouldn't believe the terrible things that people do. And they don't keep them all—they find homes for them. It's like adopting, only it's animals. And they were going to tell you, honestly they were."

Diane stuck her head in the doorway of the bedroom closest to the living room.

"No time to make the bed." Gabriella sighed. "And Duke, he is not remembering to pick up his clothes. Men! They are impossible…"

"Mom, are you listening? These animals would *die* if Duke and Gabriella didn't take them! Duke says—"

"Open that door," Diane said.

"What door?" Amelia said. "The bathroom door? King Kong—"

"I *do* know where the bathroom is in this apartment, Amelia. I seem to recall that I own this apartment. I also recall that there is another bedroom, behind *that* door, and I want to know what is in there."

"*Bien sûr*," Gabriella whispered. "Of course."

Gabriella opened the door. Amelia waited for her mother to explode.

But Diane didn't say a word. Her lips grew even tighter as her eyes swept the room.

Amelia quickly assessed the situation. Bill was asleep, and all the snakes were hidden away under their towels. Kilo was splashing happily in her pool, Apollo was grinning at them, and even her mom would have to like a red frog. "Mom, look at Winston—he's that tortoise, see? He's looking at you! He's so cool, and—"

"I've seen enough."

Gabriella sent Amelia a desperate look and closed the door.

"It is not as bad as it looks," Amelia said quickly.

"You're right. It's worse. You do know you're breaking every bylaw in the city, Gabriella."

"Pardon?" Gabriella frowned. "I do not understand."

"There's no way it can be legal to do this in the basement of someone's house. This is a residential neighborhood. We'll have the police here before you know it. Arresting all of us."

Gabriella's face brightened. "Oh, no. You must not worry about that. We have a—a paper that says we can do this."

"I suppose you mean a license. I can't imagine how you managed to get one. If you even did."

"That's a really mean thing to say," Amelia said. "Gabriella wouldn't lie. And a license means that this is okay, right?"

"No, it is absolutely not okay. Do you really think I'll be able to sleep a wink with all these creatures in the same house? You can hardly expect to keep a snake locked up in a bathroom. It'll be crawling up the pipes into our toilet. And you can close your mouth, Amelia. I've heard of that happening to someone."

"Who?" Amelia demanded.

"Someone. That snake has got to go. *All* of these animals have got to go."

"That is impossible," Gabriella said quietly. "They are our family."

Diane stared at her. "Then you and Duke will have to go."

"What?" Amelia cried. "That's not fair!"

"I'll tell you what's fair. I'll give you one week, Gabriella, *one week*, to find another place. That's more than fair. Anyone in their right mind would make you go tonight. July 1, you're gone! Then maybe I can get some proper tenants in here."

"Nobody else wants to live here, Mom!" Amelia shouted. "Did you forget that?"

"Amelia, I want you upstairs *now*."

Diane stormed through to the kitchen.

"Beaker. Beaker. Beaker," Beaker said from his cage in the corner.

Diane stopped.

"Beaker. Beaker. Beaker."

Diane walked over to the cage and pulled back a pink hand towel draped over the front. "Good Lord! What *is* that?"

"It's a bird, Mom. It's Beaker. He's a cockatiel. He can't help the way he looks. He got burned. He got under a hot tub."

"He looks bizarre. My god. Why hasn't someone put that poor thing out of his misery?"

"He is not miserable," Gabriella said stiffly. "He is just… Beaker. He has courage."

"Courage?" Diane said. "A bird?" She stared at Beaker without saying anything. Then she turned and headed to the door. "One week. That's final."

✶ ✶ ✶

Amelia heard voices in the night. Her mom and Duke. They were by the front door, and Duke was doing most of the talking. .

She had been on her way to the bathroom. She sidled down the hallway and parked herself just out of sight.

"So you see," Duke said, "I know my rights as a tenant. I've read the BC Residential Tenancy Act."

"Very impressive," Diane said. "This has obviously happened to you before. Why am I not surprised?"

"You have to give us a month's notice. It's required by law."

"Is there a section in this act on tenants misrepresenting themselves?"

"What's that supposed to mean?"

"Or how about a section on tenants harboring dangerous animals? I won't allow it, Duke. Not in my house. I don't care how many acts you've read."

"The law is the law," Duke said. "We're not going next week. We're entitled to a month's notice. I didn't want to say this, but there are penalties for landlords who break the rules. I looked it up. You could go to court. You could get *fined* even."

"Good one, Duke," Amelia whispered.

Silence.

She held her breath.

"I can print you a copy of the Act off the Internet if you want," Duke said.

Amelia heard her mother sigh. "Don't bother. Oh, all right. You're persistent, if nothing else."

"That's settled then? We have a month?"

"July 23. Not one day longer. And the deal's off if even one of those animals gets out."

"I'll tell Gabriella. She's been crying her eyes out. She's so emotional. And thank you, Diane. I really appreciate it."

"Good night, Duke."

The front door closed, and Amelia scooted back to bed.

One whole month to make her mother change her mind.

TWELVE

"Duke's mowing the lawn," Amelia said. She stood by the kitchen window, holding a bowl of Cheerios.

"I know," Diane said. "He's been at it since six o'clock this morning. It's a miracle he got the lawn mower to work. He said he fixed it with some wire he had lying around."

"This is so, *so* nice of him. Like, *really* helpful and considerate."

"Yes. Well. I offered to bring him out a coffee, but he didn't want it."

Amelia watched Duke mow a neat strip along the side of the walkway. He was wearing baggy orange shorts, a T-shirt with the sleeves torn out and a blue bandanna around his head. When he got near the house, he glanced up and waved. Amelia waved back.

"I wish you would sit down to eat your breakfast," Diane said.

"Can't. Gotta go." Amelia put her cereal bowl in the sink and grabbed her backpack.

"Amelia?"

"What?"

"I decided I was a bit…hasty yesterday. With Gabriella. The whole situation caught me by surprise. I've decided to give them a month to find somewhere else."

Amelia held back a grin. "What made you change your mind?"

"Nothing *made* me change my mind. For heaven's sake. I changed it myself. I reconsidered, that's all. Weighed all the facts."

"Oh."

"I do pride myself on keeping an open mind. No one could ever accuse me of being unbending."

"Then can you unbend a little more? And let them stay as long as they want?"

"No, I can't. I want them out by July 23. I'll be putting an ad on Craigslist for the apartment, available August 1. That'll give me a week to get the animal smell out. I'm sure we'll get someone…normal. And that's the end of it. Now off you go."

Amelia looked for Duke when she got outside, but he had disappeared around the side of the house. She heard the lawn mower sputter, roar to life, burp twice and then die. *Uh-oh.* She admired their tidy lawn and headed down the street.

Mom was wrong. The apartment smelled like vanilla. Like Gabriella.

As Amelia walked to school, she thought, Now our yard looks like everyone else's. It's not so humiliating.

Well, maybe not like the woman next door's, whose garden was a blaze of yellow, purple and pink blooms.

Amelia always stopped at the blue house near the end of their block. It was where all the cats lived. There was a low white picket fence around it and a gate in the middle. She stopped now and peered over the gate.

A tortoiseshell cat sat on the front step, washing its foot. Two black cats were sprawled across the concrete walk, sunning themselves, and a gray cat with one white front paw (Amelia's favorite) jumped up on the fence and walked toward her, purring. She rubbed it under its chin and looked up at the house. One, two, three, four cats peering out of the windows. Some days she'd counted as many as seven.

A man's face appeared behind one of the cats. He was black and had a shaved head. He watched her for a moment and then vanished.

Amelia gave the gray cat one last pat and broke into a jog. She didn't have to hurry, as there were only two days of school left and no one would care if she was late. But she wanted to get to school because she couldn't wait to tell Liam and Roshni what had happened.

At the end of the block, a girl with frizzy blond hair and long, skinny white legs in skimpy shorts was struggling to push a stroller down the sidewalk and talk on her phone at the same time. The stroller had three seats, and Amelia had never seen anything like it before. Triplets, she guessed. She smiled at the girl, but the girl was arguing with someone and kept going without even noticing her.

It wasn't the same as their old neighborhood, where everyone was friendly. Nothing in her life was the same. She made a list in her head—their poky little house, her mom tired all the time from working at Miss Jane's, hardly ever seeing Dad (not that she wanted to). And she was positive Starla was hanging out with Amber all the time now and had forgotten all about her.

She blinked back sudden tears that surprised her (she refused to cry anymore, for sure not about stuff like this) and ran the rest of the way to school.

✯ ✯ ✯

"I love doing this," Roshni said. "Here goes!"

She tipped her desk sideways, and an avalanche of crumpled papers, magazines, pencil shavings, pens and rulers crashed onto the floor.

"My April copy of *Star*!" Roshni grabbed a magazine out of the heap at her feet. She flopped down and started flipping pages. "I've been looking everywhere for this! There's the best-ever picture of Justin Bieber in here."

Amelia sat cross-legged on the floor, ignoring the commotion around her. She pulled things out of her desk and sorted them into two piles, throwaways and keepers. Most went into the throwaway pile. She had got as far as a crumpled art project of a sunset when Mr. Howard said, "Less noise in here, people. Two minutes and your desks should be emptied. Then we're all going to the gym to set up the chairs for Awards Day tomorrow."

She tossed the sunset picture onto her throwaway pile, scooped everything up and dumped it on top of an already overflowing garbage can.

"So are you guys coming to my place or not?" she said to Roshni and Liam as they headed down the hallway to the gym.

Liam was supposed to be going to his Mandarin lesson. His parents had decided it would be helpful if he could speak to his grandparents when they came from China at Christmas. Roshni still hadn't forgiven her for the science poster. And she had decided to be mad all over again when Amelia told her about Duke and Gabriella's animals. *I knew you were hiding something. I thought we were supposed to be best friends*, Roshni had said.

In her head, Amelia still gave Starla best-friend status, but she had kept her mouth shut.

Liam texted something on his phone and then said cheerfully, "My Mandarin teacher's sick. I'm coming."

"Me too." Roshni shrugged. "There's nothing else to do."

THIRTEEN

"**T**his is very, very cool," Liam said. He was kneeling beside Amelia in front of Zebra's aquarium, watching the snake twist and coil in slow circles. "He's going to do it now? For sure?"

"Yup," Duke said. "Good timing, huh? Okay. There he goes. See his head starting to come out?"

"Roshni better get in here, or she's going to miss it," Liam said.

"It won't happen that fast," Duke said.

When they'd first arrived, Roshni had wandered around the reptile room, looking at everything. Her first favorite, she'd declared, was the frog, Nate, who she insisted really did look like a ripe red tomato. Her second favorite was the little bearded dragon, Apollo. Then, before Amelia could warn her, she'd walked right up to Bill's cage. The iguana crashed against the bars with a ferocious snap of his jaws.

Roshni had screamed and leaped backward. *Thanks for the warning, Amelia*, she'd said, as if it were Amelia's fault.

She had scooted back to the living room, where Amelia could hear her talking to Gabriella. Now Amelia opened the door and shouted, "He's doing it, Roshni!"

"Can I bring the bunny?" Roshni called back.

"No," Duke said. "It's way too hot in here."

When Roshni came into the room, Liam glanced up. "I hope you're not going to talk the whole time."

"Who's talking now?" Roshni said.

Amelia ignored them. Zebra was slipping out of his old grayish-white skin. It's like he's sliding out of a sleeping bag in slow motion, she thought. A sleeping bag made out of delicate cobwebs.

They watched in silence as the snake coiled around and around the aquarium, his whole head and then his body emerging until finally he had left the old skin behind.

"He's done," Liam said. "Wow. That was fantastic."

"One of these days I'm going to make a video of that and put it on YouTube," Duke said. He reached into the aquarium and carefully picked up the discarded skin. "One of you guys want this?"

Liam looked at Amelia. "Go ahead," she said. She would have liked it, but she could tell Liam wanted it even more.

"Oh boy, thanks," Liam said. "This is great."

"I'll get you an old margarine tub to put it in," Duke said. "This is a good one. You don't always get it in one piece."

Amelia admired Zebra's gleaming new black-and-white skin and then went in search of Roshni, who had disappeared again.

She found Roshni curled up at one end of the couch, cradling Georgia, and Gabriella at the other end, clipping coupons from a printed sheet.

"Omigod, Georgia is so cute," Roshni said. "I'm going to ask my mom if I can adopt her." She stroked the bunny's soft ears. "Hey, Georgia, would you like to come and live with me?"

Liam came into the living room, holding the margarine container carefully. "I gotta go now. Are you coming, Roshni?"

"Yeah, okay." Roshni nestled the bunny beside Gabriella and stood up.

"Gabriella's going to give us a free pedicure tomorrow," she said to Amelia. "To celebrate school being over."

"Really?" Amelia had painted her fingernails once (it had all chipped off in a few days, and the color had been way too orange), but she had never done her toes. A real pedicure sounded amazing.

Gabriella shrugged. "I have no work tomorrow. Again. So it is something for me to do. You can have one too, Liam, if you want."

Liam went red. "No way. Come on, Roshni. I've got to get home."

"Okay, okay." Roshni paused. "Purple. With gold sparkles. Can you do that, Gabriella?"

Liam shoved her out the door.

✷ ✷ ✷

When they had gone, Amelia crouched beside the gecko's tank. Mary had a smiley face like Apollo's, but her eyes were different. They were big and round, like two marbles. "So what happened to Mary's tail exactly?"

"It fell off," Duke said. "Stress. She got out of her cage and hid under a couch for a week before someone found her."

"Will it grow back again?"

"Nope."

Mary's pink tongue darted out and swiped the surface of one of her eyes. "Hey," Amelia said. "What's she doing? She just licked her eye!"

"That's an eyeball kiss," Duke said. "She doesn't have any eyelids, so that's how she keeps them clean and hydrated. You can give her a drink if you want."

Mary didn't drink out of a bowl but licked droplets off leaves instead. Amelia got the spray bottle from the kitchen and lifted the wire-mesh lid of the tank. She carefully sprayed the plastic foliage.

Mary didn't move.

"I don't think she's thirsty."

"She'll drink later, when you're not watching her," Duke said. "Why don't you take Winston outside for a while?"

"Can I? Really?"

"Sure. Just take him out on the grass and let him walk around. It's good for him."

Duke trusted her. Amelia glowed.

FOURTEEN

"**I**t's me, Winston. We're going on an adventure!"

Amelia slipped her hands under the tortoise and lifted him up. His legs and head disappeared into his shell, and she whispered, "Don't be scared."

He was heavier than he looked and awkward to hold, like a bulky package. She concentrated as she carried him into the kitchen. It would be awful if she dropped him.

Gabriella was picking bright-red strawberries out of a cardboard container and washing them in the sink in a colander. If Amelia's arms hadn't been full of tortoise, she would have grabbed one.

"Strawberries from a client at the salon," Gabriella said. "Winston adores them. He can have one after his walk." She reached out and pushed the door open for Amelia.

Amelia carried Winston around to the front of the house and set him down gently in the grass. She plunked down cross-legged beside him. "Are you still in there?" she said. "Come on out. It's nice and sunny out here."

She saw the tip of Winston's head first. Slowly it poked out of his shell, his tiny eyes blinking, followed by his stubby legs.

His head swiveled back and forth on his long, papery neck. Then he set off at a steady but very slow ramble across the lawn.

"Not so close to the sidewalk," Amelia said. She picked him up and carried him back to the middle of the lawn. She thought it was a good sign that he wanted to explore. She wasn't sure, but she figured a tortoise that was getting sick might just huddle there.

"You're feeling okay, right, Winston? You're not getting sick or anything?" She turned him so he was facing the house. "Go that way."

Winston took a few steps and then veered back toward the street. Amelia crawled after him on her hands and knees and scooped him up. "You are one stubborn tortoise! Do you want a car to hit you or something?"

She stuck her legs out straight and tucked Winston in between them. He settled down to nibble grass. She ran her fingers gently over the bumps on his shell. He felt amazing. She wished someone would walk by and see them, but the street was quiet except for the distant drone of a lawn mower.

Finally she got up and said, "Strawberries! Come on. Let's go in!"

She carried Winston inside and settled him back on his bed of hay. Then she went to the kitchen to get a strawberry.

"Cut it into pieces," Gabriella said. "It is easier for him to eat it that way. And take some for yourself."

It was fun watching Winston eat the strawberry pieces. He stretched his head forward, and Amelia could see his pink tongue. Every time he gobbled up a piece, she said, "Score!" and popped a juicy berry in her mouth.

After she left Winston, with a promise to take him out again soon, she hung around for a while, helping Gabriella with her coupons.

"Three coupons for Revlon under-eye night cream. It is not something I need, of course." Gabriella sighed. "Half price. It is such a good deal. Someone should use them."

"Mom might. She's always complaining about the bags under her eyes."

"This is very good then." Gabriella handed them to Amelia. "She can take them to Shoppers. And here is a coupon for an avocado face pack. She is on holidays, right? She should pamper herself."

"Thanks." Amelia stood up and stretched. "I guess I better go. I'm just going to say goodbye to Beaker."

Beaker's head was tucked under his wing. A few sparse white hairs stuck up, and flakes of dandruff speckled his scrawny neck. A string of shiny yellow, red and blue wooden beads dangled in the corner of his cage. "Hey, Beaker's got a new toy," she said.

"Your mom bought it."

"*My* mom did? You're kidding."

"She thought it would cheer him up. She went to Pets Plus. She still does not believe that Beaker is happy."

Amelia stared at Beaker. Just like that, an amazingly brilliant plan popped into her head. She examined the idea and thought, Bingo! Her mom was spending the afternoon at Jeannie's house, practicing massages, so the coast was clear.

"Can I borrow Beaker?"

FIFTEEN

Duke helped Amelia set Beaker up in their kitchen. They put the cage close to the window, so he could see outside. "Make sure the window stays closed to keep the drafts off him," Duke said. He attached a heat lamp to the side of the cage and ran an extension cord to the socket near the floor.

"So tell me again how this plan of yours is going to work," he said.

"Mom will fall in love with Beaker, and then she'll change her mind and let you stay because she won't want you to take Beaker away. I *know* she will."

"I hope so. Okay, that looks good. I'm off." Duke paused. "Are you doing anything later?"

"No."

"I'm going to Kerrisdale to pick up a lizard. D'you want to come?"

Kerrisdale. Amelia's heart jumped. Her old neighborhood. Her old house. Starla. Dad and his girlfriend-wife and the twins and the baby.

"Um…"

"You don't have to."

Kerrisdale wasn't that big, but it was big enough that they probably wouldn't drive down her street. And going out with Duke would be so much fun. "I want to."

"Perfect. Simon's picking me up in about an hour. We're going in his van." Duke tapped the birdcage lightly. "See you, Beaker. Be good."

Amelia hung around watching Beaker until her mother came home. Diane came into the kitchen and dropped a white paper bag from the bakery on the table. "Jelly donuts. One each. I've been very good, so no comments from the peanut gallery, please." She spotted Beaker and raised her eyebrows. "What's all this about?"

Amelia had her story ready. "We thought Beaker was lonely, 'cause Duke's been going out a lot lately, picking up animals and stuff, and Gabriella's at the salon lots of days. And since you're on holidays now, well, we thought you could keep him company."

"That's right, *holidays.* I'm not babysitting a bird."

"Not babysit. Just talk to him a bit. Just when you're here. It's not like we expect you to stay home all the time."

"Well, thank you for that." Diane glanced at the coupons that Amelia had left on the counter. "Where'd these come from?"

"They're from Gabriella. They're for you." Amelia opened the bakery bag and took out a sugary donut that was leaking red jelly. "This can be my dinner. I'm going with Duke to pick up a lizard."

Before Diane could protest, Amelia fled outside. She sat on the lawn, eating her donut and licking the sugar off her fingers.

When Simon's rusty van pulled up, Amelia darted inside to tell her mom she was going. Diane was standing beside Beaker's cage. "Are you being a good boy, Beaker? Yes, yes, you are. Very good."

Amelia grinned and left.

"You owe me one, bro," Simon said, as Duke settled into the front seat of the van. "I've got a ton of studying to do tonight."

"Yeah, yeah. You remember Amelia?"

Simon swung around and peered at Amelia in the backseat. "The kid from upstairs, right?"

"We're going to 5375 Balsam Street," Duke said. "It's an apartment building."

Amelia's old house was on 36th Avenue, which ran into Balsam. She wasn't sure about the numbers. How close was 5375 to her old street? For a second she wondered if she should jump out of the van. But then Simon pulled away from the curb, and it was too late. He sped through Burnaby and across the city to Kerrisdale.

Duke draped his arm over the back of his seat and described the lizard they were picking up. "It's called a green basilisk lizard. Some people call them Jesus Christ lizards 'cause when they get scared they can run across the surface of the water. They've got these fringes between their back toes. They can run for fifteen feet before they sink, and then they can stay under water for half an hour."

"It never fails to amaze me how much useless information you know, bro." Simon beeped his horn. "Idiot! Ever hear of signaling?"

"It's not useless," Amelia said.

Duke grinned at her. "Basilisk lizards can get pretty long, but it's mostly tail."

"How long?"

"Two feet or so. But they don't weigh very much. This one belongs to someone called Doris. She's moving. She sounded pretty upset on the phone."

"Have you ever seen one run across the water?" Amelia said.

"No. They do that in the wild. They drop out of trees."

"Have you ever had one before?"

"Yup. One. His name was Verde, which means 'green' in Spanish. He was caught in the jungle in Costa Rica, which is totally illegal. When we got him, one of his eyeballs was poked out. I'm pretty sure there must have been wires sticking out in the cage he was shipped in."

"Did he die?"

"No. He was pretty bad, but he got better. He's in a good home now."

"What about his eye?"

"I sewed the socket shut. To keep the dirt out."

"Spare us the details," Simon said. "Could everyone kind of pay attention? I don't want to drive around all night looking for this street."

"I know where it is," Amelia said. She watched carefully out the window. "We're getting close. Turn at that light and go down the Boulevard. And then you can go along 37th Avenue, and that'll take you to Balsam."

Now they were on 37th Avenue. One block from 36th. She spotted the Mac's convenience store on the corner, where she and Starla used to buy slushies, and the neat old church on the corner of Larch Street and 37th Avenue. She could walk to her old house in two minutes from here.

"Here's Balsam," Simon said. "Start looking at the numbers."

Amelia spotted the apartment building first, set back in leafy green shrubs.

Simon muttered that he would wait in the van, and Duke and Amelia went inside. They climbed the stairs to the third floor. "Here it is," Duke said. "Number 302." He rang the doorbell. There was a series of mysterious thumps and dragging sounds, and then, just when Amelia whispered, "What's going on?" a chain rattled and the door opened a crack.

A tiny woman with fluffy white hair, wearing a pink tracksuit and leaning against a walker, peered out. "Oh my," she said. "Oh goodness, you're much too early."

"I said seven o'clock," Duke said.

"Eight o'clock," Doris said in a quivery voice. "Oh dear, I'm not ready. But you'd better come in."

She slid the chain back with fumbling fingers and opened the door.

The apartment was hot and stuffy and full of spindly furniture. The lizard was in a huge glass aquarium in the tiny living room. Amelia looked at the creature with interest. It was slim and green and had three ridges that stuck up on its back. The aquarium was amazing, with twisty branches for climbing on and a miniature pond surrounded by plastic flowers. Two large bulbs were attached to the ends.

"I haven't even packed Oliver's things yet," Doris said. "I'm sure you said eight." Her eyes filled with tears. "I'm just not ready."

"No problem," Duke said. "We'll come back in an hour. It sucks to say goodbye. You take your time, Doris. Just take your time."

SIXTEEN

"**W**hat?" Simon exploded.

"She's an old lady," Duke said. "You can tell she loves Oliver. She's probably moving into an old folks' home or something."

Simon pulled a textbook out of a backpack on the van floor. "Old ladies aren't supposed to like lizards. And I need quiet to study."

"Amelia and I will walk up to 41st. There's gotta be a Starbucks or something up there."

There *was* a Starbucks. Amelia knew that for sure. She and her dad used to go there every Saturday afternoon. She'd order a hot chocolate and her dad a cafe mocha, and they'd get a cinnamon bun to share. They'd take it to the same table in the back corner.

Amelia always ate the whipped cream with a spoon while her hot chocolate cooled, and her dad read emails on his iPhone and gulped his coffee. She didn't care that they didn't exactly talk. And when her dad always pretended that she'd taken the biggest half of the cinnamon bun, she'd grin even though she wondered if he thought she was still six years old.

Amelia thought she would be okay. It was just a Starbucks, after all. But she felt weird when they got to the door. It was familiar and not familiar, like she was coming back from a long voyage. She followed Duke inside. It was packed with people, and they joined the back of the line, behind three giggly teenage girls.

"Have whatever you want," Duke said. "It's on me."

Amelia studied the board. "A cinnamon dolce latte." Roshni always talked about lattes, and Amelia didn't like to admit she'd never had one.

While she waited, she glanced over at the corner table.

A silver-haired man was sitting between two little girls, laughing at something one of them had said. Then he picked up a crayon and drew on a piece of paper.

He glanced up and saw Amelia staring at him.

He stood up and called out something. She thought he might be saying, "What a surprise, Amelia!" or "It's not what it looks like, Amelia!"

She didn't wait to find out. She turned and ran, out the door and onto the street. She raced down 41st Avenue, tears spilling down her cheeks as she dodged around pedestrians.

It was their table. Their tradition. How could he?

Her tears turned into sobs. As she turned onto Balsam, a woman getting out of a parked car said, "Are you all right?"

She kept running. When Simon's van came into sight, she stopped and scrubbed her cheeks with the palms of her hands. She wanted to duck into the bushes beside the apartment building until Duke came back, but Simon glanced up and gave her a nod. She felt she had no choice but to get in the van.

She climbed onto the cracked vinyl backseat and stared at her knees. She could feel Simon watching her in the rearview mirror. Her face must look awful, red and blotchy.

"Please don't look at me," she mumbled.

"Gotcha," Simon said.

For the next few minutes, the only sound was Simon flipping pages. Amelia didn't feel like crying anymore. She felt empty and drained inside, like a squeezed-out sponge.

"Can I open a window back here?" she said. "It's boiling."

"They don't work."

"Oh." Amelia slid forward so her bare legs wouldn't stick to the hot vinyl seat. She peered down the street as far as she could. Where was Duke? Was he going to be furious?

She caught Simon's eye in the rearview mirror, and he said, "Oops, I'm not supposed to look at you."

Amelia felt herself smile. "I'm all right now. It was just the shock."

"Right."

She sighed. "My dad dumped me for another family."

"Ouch," Simon said. "That's harsh."

She told him the whole story. It spilled out of her. Even though Simon wasn't as nice as Duke, she had to admit he was an awesome listener. When she got to the end, she said,

"I don't even know if he wants to get a divorce. And I don't know if I care."

"Hmmm," Simon said. "You know what? There's something to be said for the Mosuo's approach to fatherhood."

"What?"

"The Mosuo. They live in the Himalayas in China. The mothers rear their kids. No dads involved. They don't even have a word for father."

"How do you know that?"

"I'm an anthropology major. I'm supposed to know stuff like that."

"Is that true really? The fathers don't have anything to do with their kids?"

"True." Simon grinned. "You can google it if you don't believe me. It's spelled *m-o-s-u-o*."

Just then Duke tapped at the van door with his foot. He was juggling three paper cups with lids.

Simon leaned over and pushed the door open.

"A latte for the lady and two cappuccinos," Duke said.

Duke didn't say one word about her running away, which was very cool. Amelia pressed her feet in her lime-green flip-flops against the back of Duke's seat. She sipped the latte (delicious!) and examined her toenails. Tomorrow was the pedicure. Lime green, she decided, to match her flip-flops.

When they were finished, Duke said, "Time to go get Oliver. I need you to help me carry the aquarium, Si."

"I'm your slave now too?" Simon grumbled. "Not just a taxi driver?"

As he slung himself out of the van, he winked at Amelia.

When Amelia got home, she googled Mosuo on the laptop. She clicked on a National Geographic article. *Remote Group Has No Dads, And Never Did,* the headline said.

Simon was right. Most Mosuo kids didn't even know who their dads were. *By most accounts, children seem to do just fine under this arrangement,* she read.

She'd better tell Liam about this. He'd probably end up being an expert on the Mosuo. She clicked on another site with a bunch of information on division of chores and something called extended families, but it was boring and hard to understand.

The National Geographic site was the best, so she went back to it.

The article ended with a quote: *"The society does kind of create this question: Are fathers really necessary?"*

She sighed. How should she know? She turned off the laptop and headed downstairs.

SEVENTEEN

Gabriella was sitting at the kitchen table, staring at a sea of scraps of paper. Not coupons this time, Amelia noticed. Receipts, like from a grocery store or a drugstore.

Gabriella punched some buttons on a small calculator. "*Merde!* What is Duke thinking?" She scribbled a number on a piece of yellow paper that was already covered with rows of numbers. "Help yourself to a drink," she said.

Amelia found some cans of Coke and Sprite on the bottom shelf of the fridge. The rest of the fridge was taken up by a pizza box, a carton of orange juice and at least a dozen containers of peach yogurt.

"That's a lot of yogurt," she said. "Coupons?"

"Three for the price of one."

Duke came into the kitchen as she was grabbing a can of Sprite. He reached over her, picked up the carton of orange juice, tipped it back and took a long drink.

Gabriella watched him.

"What?" Duke said.

"You drink orange juice like it is water. It does not come out of a tap."

"Your point?"

"We are out of money again. *C'est impossible!* You are spending too much."

"So we don't buy orange juice. We'll live on yogurt."

"It is not funny!" Gabriella grabbed a handful of receipts. "Look at this. All this in one month! Six new UV lightbulbs! One hundred and eighty dollars!"

"They burn out," Duke said.

"A hammock! Fifteen dollars!"

"The ferrets needed one."

"Gecko food, timothy hay, water conditioner, turtle pellets, a heat lamp…" Gabriella's voice rose. "I am down to two days at the salon. Two days! And probably next month no days! And we have more rent to pay in one week."

She glanced at Amelia. Just for a second. As if maybe, possibly, Amelia could do something about the rent. But she couldn't, she thought miserably. Her mom would be furious if Duke and Gabriella didn't pay the rent for their last three weeks. It would be absolutely the last straw. She'd kick them out right away.

"You need to charge more for your…what do you call them? Consultations," Gabriella said. "You help all these people with their problems, but you do not ask for enough money."

"I ask as much as I can. I'm not a vet." Duke sank into a chair beside Gabriella. "The frozen rats are being delivered tomorrow," he said quietly.

"How much?" Gabriella said.

"Two hundred dollars."

"*Mon dieu!*"

"I had to order some jumbos for King Kong. They're expensive."

"And why is Pia not paying for this?"

"She will. As soon as she has the money."

"She should pay now," Gabriella muttered. "You are too easy."

"Okay, okay. I'll look on Craigslist. I'll find a night job at a gas station or a 7-Eleven."

Gabriella's face instantly softened. "But you work so hard all day. These animals take all your time."

"It doesn't matter. I don't want to close down our business."

Amelia froze. *Close the business.* Was he serious? What would happen to Winston? Beaker? All the other animals? Gabriella was right when she told Diane that the animals were their family. My family too, she thought, realizing with a sudden stab how much the animals meant to her. She couldn't bear to see them go.

She slipped out of the kitchen and into the reptile room. She crouched down beside Winston's box and stared into his tiny black eyes.

What was he thinking about? Did he like hanging out with her? Or was he just in his own tortoise world?

She decided she would ask Duke his opinion. He would know.

She stood up and whispered, "Good night, Winston." A sudden lump filled her throat. She had promised Winston that Gabriella and Duke would look after him, that he would never end up in a drainage ditch again. How was she going to keep that promise?

EIGHTEEN

"*Voilà!*" Gabriella said. "*C'est fini!*"

"Perfect," Amelia said. She and Roshni were sitting side by side on kitchen chairs. She stuck her legs out and admired her toes. She had found the exact lime green she had wanted among Gabriella's assorted bottles of nail polish. Roshni had picked black in the end, and when Amelia had asked her why, she'd looked mysterious. Copying some star in one of her magazines, Amelia had thought with a grin.

"How long do we have to keep the cotton balls between our toes?" Roshni said.

"Fifteen minutes. And then you can get up, but make sure you wear your flip-flops. Sneakers will smudge the polish."

Gabriella's phone rang, and she picked it up. "No, he is not here…What?…What?…Oh…I guess so, yeah, I will tell him…"

She frowned. "*Merde!* That was that woman from the community center. Duke was supposed to do a show there next week for the kids' camp, and he would have got a hundred bucks for it, but they are going to cancel. So many kids are sick. Colds! *C'est incroyable!* How do children get colds in the summer? That would not happen in France."

Duke came in the door, carrying a metal cage. He set it on the floor and said, "Someone brought it back to the pet store. They can't resell it, so they said I could take it for free." He glanced at the girls. "Cool toes."

He wandered into the living room and came back with Lysander cradled against his chest. Gabriella was arranging her bottles of nail polish in rows in their box, but Amelia didn't think she was really paying attention—she was banging the same bottles around in circles. Gabriella looked up at Duke and said, "So?"

"I was too late for the Tim Hortons job. They hired someone already this morning." Lysander crept up onto Duke's shoulder and nibbled his ear. "Hey, kisses only, Lysander!"

"So that is it," Gabriella said.

"No," Duke said, prying Lysander off his shoulder. He rolled him over on the palm of his hand and rubbed his white tummy. "I went all over the place. The guy at the Husky on Boundary said I *might* get the graveyard shift on the weekends, but I have to wait till the manager gets there. He said he'd call me later today."

"*Might*," Gabriella said tightly. "And today that woman from the community center phones—"

Amelia pulled the cotton balls out from between her toes and slid into her flip-flops. "Come on, Roshni," she whispered. "Let's go."

When Roshni was ready, Amelia closed the door softly behind them. She hated listening to Gabriella and Duke fight about money. It made her feel mixed up inside. Freaked out and helpless, all at the same time.

✷ ✷ ✷

Roshni flopped on Amelia's bed and said, "*Graveyard* shift? What does that mean? It sounds spooky."

"It just means working at night." Amelia was sometimes shocked at the things Roshni didn't know. "Gabriella and Duke are broke."

"Oh. Like, really broke?"

"Yeah."

Roshni pulled a magazine out of her backpack and propped herself up against the pillow. Amelia walked to her window and looked down at the street. At the house right across from them, a woman with a blond ponytail was hanging laundry on a clothesline. A long row of T-shirts and blue jeans that looked like they had been spattered with white paint. Amelia had seen her before, climbing into the truck parked in front of her house that said *Rachel's Renos—No Job Too Small.*

The woman with the triplet stroller wheeled past, hunched over as if she were on a mission. Amelia thought she might stop and say hi to Rachel, but she didn't. That's what it was like here. Nobody talked to anybody.

In her old neighborhood, Starla's mom always organized a barbecue on the last day of school, right in their front yard, and everyone brought lawn chairs, salads and drinks. People would spread across the grass and onto the sidewalk. It was probably going on right now.

"If we had a barbecue here, no one would come," Amelia said.

"Huh?" Roshni said.

"Nothing." Amelia flopped into her beanbag chair and admired her toes again.

"Okay. Listen to this," Roshni said. "*Smokin' Mirrors. Made in more than one shade! Celebs brighten their days with Ray-Ban's mirrored aviators.*" She turned the magazine toward Amelia. "Don't they look fantastic? That's Hilary Duff."

"I know what Hilary Duff looks like," Amelia said.

"They come in blue, green and orange. Green, Amelia. They could match your toes. It says you can get them at sunglasshut.com." She paused. "Oh."

"What?"

"A little pricey. One hundred and fifty bucks. We could collect pop cans or something."

"I wouldn't waste a hundred and fifty bucks on sunglasses! A hundred and fifty bucks would probably buy a brand-new aquarium. Or ten bags of gecko food. Or six UV bulbs!" Roshni was staring at her with her mouth open, but Amelia kept going. "A month's supply of frozen rats!"

Roshni reached into her backpack and pulled out another magazine. She tossed it to Amelia. "Read."

Amelia flipped the magazine open to the middle. In big block letters at the top of the page, it said, CELEBS PUT ANIMALS' BEST INTERESTS FIRST. Photos of celebrities and their pets were spread in a collage across two pages— Angelina Jolie with a dog with a squished-in face, Taylor Swift with a cat, Justin Bieber with a little white dog, Britney Spears holding some kind of parrot, Jennifer Aniston with a German shepherd, Lady Gaga with a poodle.

There were other celebrities Amelia didn't know—a woman with a snake and a man with…*wait a sec*. A *ferret* on a leash! It looked a bit like The Accountant.

Her eyes stopped on a photo of a man holding a tortoise. "Roshni, look at this." She hopped up onto the bed. "These are all celebrities' pets, and that guy has a sulcata tortoise. I'm positive it's a sulcata tortoise! It's identical to Winston."

Roshni peered at the magazine. "That's not just some *guy*. That's Leonardo DiCaprio."

"Whatever. This is interesting."

Dotted among the photos were captions and blurbs of information. Amelia read bits out loud to Roshni. "Nicolas Cage has a king cobra called Sheba, and Charlie Sheen has a Chinese water dragon! Lady Gaga's poodle is called Fozzi. Justin Bieber supports something called PETA, which means—it says here at the bottom—People for the Ethical Treatment of Animals. And Simon Cowell likes something called the World Society for the Protection of Animals."

She took a big breath. "Wow."

"What's so wow?" Roshni said.

"I just didn't think famous rich people would care about stuff like that."

"It's good PR."

"No, I think they really do care. Oh! Jennifer Aniston's dog came from the Best Friends Animal Society." Amelia felt excitement growing inside her in leaps and bounds. "Roshni, I'm positive it was fate that I turned to this page. We could write to them. Ask them for donations for Duke and Gabriella. Duke's got a website and an official name and everything, so they'd know it wasn't a fake."

Roshni stared at Amelia. "Like, email them?"

"Well, yeah."

Just then Diane tapped on Amelia's door.

"Don't tell Mom about this," Amelia said. She shouted, "Come in!"

Diane opened the door and poked her head inside. "Hello, Roshni. I didn't know you were here. How was Awards Day?"

"Boring," Roshni said.

"Well that's too bad." Diane turned to Amelia. "We've just been invited, spur of the moment, to a barbecue. I want you to get ready. We'll go in about twenty minutes. Sorry to kick you out, Roshni."

"Starla's mom phoned?" Amelia said.

Diane looked surprised. "No. Why would she phone? Jeannie's invited us. She and Frank are getting a bunch of people together, and she said there'll be some other kids your age."

Great. She wouldn't know one person there (Frank didn't count), and she'd have to listen to Jeannie laugh her head off at everything her mother said. And she was dying to get started on this celebrity thing.

Roshni jumped off the bed, scooped up her magazines and stuffed them into her backpack. "I'm outta here. I'll ask Liam. He's got a computer in his bedroom we could use."

"Thanks!" Amelia said.

"See you tomorrow."

When Roshni had gone, Diane said, "That's ridiculous, a twelve-year-old boy with his own computer in his room. Don't his parents realize how many predators are out there?" She paused in the doorway. "And what do you need Liam's computer for anyway?"

"Nothing." Amelia looked at her mother. "*What?*"

"We're leaving in twenty minutes," Diane said and left.

NINETEEN

"The first thing," Liam said, "is you can't email celebrities." He was sitting at his desk in his bedroom, his chair tipped back, waiting for his computer to fire up. Amelia and Roshni stood behind him, staring at the screen.

"Why not?" Roshni said.

"Because you can't get their email addresses. It's a privacy thing. Why would they want to be bugged with thousands of emails every day? And it would totally over-load their inboxes. Nope. Not going to work."

The annoying thing was, Liam was usually right about stuff. "So what are we supposed to do?" Amelia said.

"Write letters."

"Are you serious?" Roshni said. "You mean, like, on a piece of paper?"

"Snail mail," Liam said cheerfully.

"Great," Amelia said. "It will take forever. And we need the money fast."

"The second thing," Liam continued, "is they won't send money anyway."

"Liam," Roshni snapped, "are you with us or not?"

Liam shrugged. "I'm just telling you the truth. Celebrities get sick of being asked for donations."

Roshni leaned over his shoulder and grabbed the mouse. She clicked on Google, typed in *Writing to Celebrities* and clicked *Search*.

"Look at all the sites!" she crowed. "If this was such a dumb idea, why are there so many sites about it?"

"Click on Contactinganycelebrity.com," Amelia said.

The first thing that came up was *NEED TO CONTACT A CELEBRITY?* in bold letters. "There's a video," Roshni said. "Cool." She clicked on the starting arrow.

The video made Amelia think of a space movie. The background was starry, and captions zoomed in and out with *Star Wars*-y kind of music. *NEED TO CONTACT A CELEBRITY? NOW YOU CAN! 60,000 + CELEBRITIES + PUBLIC FIGURES. WHAT ARE YOU WAITING FOR? START MY FREE 14-DAY TRIAL NOW!*

"Should we do it?" she said.

"Sure!" Roshni clicked on the Free Trial link.

Pictures of credit cards—Visa, MasterCard—flashed on the screen.

"Big surprise!" Liam said. "They always want your money!"

"I don't suppose your dad gave you a credit card too," Amelia said.

"Not yet. Not that I'd let you use it anyway. "

"Okay," Roshni said. "We find a site that really is free. All we need are some addresses for the celebrities. It's not like we want to buy something."

No one was faster with a mouse than Roshni, so Amelia just watched. Liam watched too. He was bouncing a tennis ball against the wall and pretending *not* to watch, but Amelia saw his eyes darting across the room to the screen.

"Okay," Roshni said. "Here's one. Fanmail.biz. Perfect. Let's try it out. Give me a name. Any name."

"Taylor Swift," Amelia said.

"Coming up." Roshni's fingers flew. "Here it is! Taylor Swift Entertainment, 242 West Main Street, Hendersonville, Tennessee 37075, USA."

"That sounds like a real address," Amelia said.

"Of course it's a real address."

The girls spun around and grinned at Liam.

"I never said you couldn't write to celebrities," Liam said. "I was actually the one who said you'd have to write letters. I just said they won't send you any money."

"Give me a piece of paper out of your printer," Amelia said. "I'll start writing them down."

One hour later, Amelia and Roshni had a list of fifteen names and addresses:

Justin Bieber
Angelina Jolie
Taylor Swift
Matt Damon
Lady Gaga

Jennifer Aniston
Madonna
Britney Spears
Simon Cowell
Leonardo DiCaprio
Nicolas Cage
Charlie Sheen
Oprah
Dr. Phil
J.K. Rowling

J.K. Rowling had been Liam's idea. *You might as well go after the big bucks*, he'd said.

Amelia read the list out loud. "Now we've got to figure out what to say."

"WikiHow." Liam produced a folded piece of paper from his pocket. "'How to Write a Fan Letter.' I printed it before you got here."

"I knew it! I *knew* it!" Roshni said. "Admit it, Liam. You think this is going to work!"

"I just don't want you guys to make fools of yourself. D'you want to hear this or not?"

"Shoot," Amelia said.

"*Number one*," Liam read. "*Start by giving a two- to three-sentence intro about yourself. Include basic details such as your first name, what country/town you're from and your age. Number two, explain how you got to know about them. A friend? Radio? Television show? Number three—*"

"This is so obvious," Amelia said. "Let's just start."

"Patience." Liam glanced at the girls' faces. "Okay, okay, I'll skip to the important stuff. Let's see… *Compliment them. Tell them you liked their outfit at the Grammys. Mention that you'll be hoping for a response. You could consider saying something along the lines of 'If you could find some time, I'd appreciate it, but I'll understand if you don't.'*"

"Forget it!" Roshni protested. "That'll just give them an excuse."

Liam continued reading. "*Don't make up a story, such as saying you'll die in a month and the only way to cheer you up would be to hear from them.*"

"Why are you looking at me?" Roshni said.

"*Use 'Yours sincerely' or 'From your biggest fan' with your name. Do not use 'Lots of love'—it may scare the celebrity out of writing back. And try to refrain from saying things like 'I love you! You're so hot! Will you marry me?' It's freaky.*" He paused. "I like the *It's freaky* part."

"Okay, we get it," Amelia said. "Can we use some of your printer paper, Liam? We need fifteen sheets."

"Can't we at least type this on the computer?" Roshni said. "We could do one letter and then just fill in names and stuff."

"Too impersonal," Liam said.

"Well, I'm not going to handwrite it," Roshni said. "Handwriting sucks."

"We can print." Liam opened his desk drawer and took out a handful of pens.

Amelia noticed that Liam said *we*, but she kept her mouth shut. "Everyone should write a practice letter," she said. "And we'll pick the best one."

"One more thing," Liam said. "It says here that *just because a few days, weeks, months or even a whole year might pass without a reply, this doesn't mean you'll never get—*"

"Shut up and write," Roshni said.

* * *

In the end, they used a little bit of everybody's letter. When they had put everything together, Amelia read it out loud.

Dear BLANK,

We'd like to introduce ourselves. Our names are Amelia, Roshni and Liam. We live in Vancouver. We are devoted fans of yours. We love your new BLANK.

Option one: We think you looked awesome at the BLANK awards. Congratulations on winning!

Option two: We think you looked awesome at the BLANK awards. We think you should have won.

Option three: We can't understand why you have never been nominated for a BLANK award, because you totally deserve it.

We have heard that you love animals as much as we do. Your pet BLANK sounds awesome.

Are you looking for a new worthy cause? Please consider DUKE'S DEN (dukesden.com). Duke and Gabriella devote their lives to saving unwanted animals. They NEED your support!!! Checks can be made out to Duke's Den and sent to the return address on this envelope.

ANIMALS DESERVE OUR HELP! If you could find some time to reply, we would appreciate it.

Your biggest fans,
Amelia, Roshni and Liam

"It sounds pretty good," Roshni said.

"Not bad," Liam said. "I'll do the research for the blanks and you guys can start writing the letters." Roshni opened her mouth to protest, and Liam added, "Hey, it's *my* computer."

Liam called out bits of information as the girls wrote. He got sidetracked reading reviews out loud for Matt Damon's latest movie ("Drop it and find out what color Angelina Jolie's dress was at the Oscars!" Roshni demanded), but in less than an hour they were done.

Liam found envelopes in his mother's desk, and they addressed them carefully and slid their letters into them.

"What about stamps?" Roshni said.

"Dad's picking me up at one," Liam said. "He'll mail them for us. I'll talk him into sending them express."

Amelia scooped up the envelopes and handed them to Liam. "Thanks!"

"I still say they won't send money."

"They will," Amelia said.

TWENTY

"You're just in time," Duke said.

"For what?"

Amelia had decided not to tell Duke and Gabriella about the celebrity thing until the first check came. She wanted it to be a surprise. But when she glanced at Gabriella rummaging through her shoe box of coupons as she scribbled on a shopping list, it was hard not to give even a hint. *Face cream, bath oils and night revitalizing cream for your mom,* Gabriella had said when Amelia walked in, handing her some coupons. *And does your mom use Tide? I have too many coupons for Tide.*

Yeah, she does. Thanks.

Amelia peered over Duke's shoulder at a fat white rat, lying on its back at the bottom of a bowl of water, staring up at her. "Oh yuck. Double yuck. What are you doing?"

"Thawing it out."

"What are you going to do with it?"

"Feed it to King Kong." Duke poked the rat with his finger. "It's done. D'you want to watch?"

"I think so." The rat was dead, after all. Very dead. "Okay. I do. Liam said you're supposed to feed *live* rats to snakes. He saw it on YouTube."

"Some people do. But it's risky. If the snake isn't hungry and doesn't look out, the rat will try to eat the snake. I've seen snakes chewed up pretty bad."

King Kong was curled up in the corner of his cage, his head tucked under one of his coils. "He looks like he's asleep," Amelia said.

"He'll get interested pretty fast," Duke said. "Pia said he hasn't eaten for a month."

Duke picked up a pair of tongs and wrapped a towel around his arm. "Just in case. I don't want him to bite me. He's usually pretty gentle but not when food is around."

He grabbed the limp, soggy rat with the tongs. Amelia kept her eyes riveted on King Kong. Duke opened the cage door and dangled the white rat in front of the snake.

Amelia leaped back as King Kong's head darted out, lightning fast, and struck at the rat.

"Scary?" Duke said. He closed the cage door.

"A bit," she admitted. She watched King Kong wrap himself around the limp white body. Then he was very still.

"Doesn't he want it?"

"He's strangling it as if it were live prey. He's a constrictor, and that's what they do. He'll stay like that for about ten minutes. Then he'll eat it. I've got stuff to do, but you can stay in here if you want. While you're waiting for some action, you can mist Oliver's tank."

Amelia poured water from a water bottle into the mister. (*Never use tap water*, Duke had told her, *because of the chlorine.*) She peered into Oliver's tank and spotted him sprawled along a branch. She thought he was one of the prettiest lizards, with his bright emerald-green skin and handsome crests. She carefully sprayed the walls of the tank and the plastic foliage. She had asked Duke if he thought Oliver missed his former owner, Doris, but he had said, *Probably not. Basilisk lizards aren't really social with people. They actually hate being handled.*

Next she checked on Apollo, the little brown bearded dragon. His story made her feel sick. Duke had got him from a woman whose son went off to university. "She just stuck him in a cupboard! He was living in complete darkness. It's critical that bearded dragons have full-spectrum lighting. Sunlight. But when I told her where to get a UV bulb, she said it sounded too complicated. Thanks to her, he's got a bone disease."

Duke knew so much. He was like an animal encyclopedia. Every time Amelia talked to him, she learned something new.

She glanced over at King Kong. Still nothing happening. She visited with Winston for a few minutes (he was basking under his heat lamp and seemed content to be left alone) and then settled herself in front of King Kong's cage.

She didn't have to wait long. King Kong twisted his head and nudged the rat's nose. *It almost looks like he's licking it*, she thought. She watched, fascinated, as the snake pushed at the rat. Finally, the snake's mouth gaped open and clamped around the rat's head.

Duke slipped into the room and stood behind her. "His jaws are hinged," he said. "That's why he can open his mouth so wide."

King Kong slowly sucked the rat's head into his mouth, his jaws moving in and out, in and out.

Amelia felt queasy watching. "Is he chewing it?" she asked as the rat's head gradually disappeared.

"He's swallowing it whole," Duke said.

How was there room for a whole rat to fit inside King Kong? But then the snake started to swell and thicken. "See his muscles squeezing?" Duke said. "He's squishing the rat and kind of compacting it. He'll get faster as he goes along."

Ripples moved under King Kong's skin as he drew the rat inside his powerful body. When all Amelia could see were the rat's two scrawny back legs and a skinny white tail sticking out, the snake raised his head. She held her breath as the tip of the rat's tail disappeared.

Then King Kong opened his mouth wide in a great big yawn.

"He's resetting his jaw," Duke said as the snake rested his head back down on the cage floor. "We'll leave him alone now for a couple of days. And then he'll be back to his old friendly self." He grinned at Amelia. "Not too gory?"

"No. It's nature, right?"

"Yup. It's nature. Just don't tell Zak and Lysander."

✮ ✮ ✮

"Jeannie called with that phone number," Diane said after dinner.

"What number?" Amelia was rinsing spaghetti sauce off their plates and stacking them in the dishwasher.

"Maybe you didn't hear her. Last night at the party. Her niece lives in Langley and just got a job for a year in Thailand. She's looking for someone to rent her house."

Amelia went still inside.

"I told her about Duke and Gabriella, and Jeannie said that Angie, that's her niece, is a real animal lover and that they should give her a call. She's pretty sure Angie wouldn't mind all the animals."

Amelia didn't say anything while her mother rummaged through some papers on the counter by the phone. "Here it is." Diane produced a used envelope with a phone number scrawled across it. "This could be a perfect solution. It's very nice in Langley. Very rural still. And it's a whole house. Way better for an animal refuge."

Amelia knew where Langley was. Starla's dad had taken her and Starla to Fort Langley once. It was miles and miles away. She would never see Duke and Gabriella again. She hated how her mother was pretending to care what happened to them.

She grabbed the envelope from Diane's hand. "I'll give it to them."

TWENTY-ONE

Amelia slid the envelope out of sight under her beanbag chair. She called Roshni, but Roshni's mom said that her dad had taken her and her two sisters to Playland. Liam was out too, with his dad.

She sighed. What was *her* dad doing right now? Something with those twins or that new baby, she bet.

She wandered into the living room. Diane was flipping channels on the TV while Beaker scuttled around on the coffee table, whistling softly. "There's a special on tonight about Queen Elizabeth," Diane said. "Her birthday celebration was last Saturday. Not her real birthday, of course. That was in April."

"So why do they celebrate it in June?" Amelia slumped on the couch and reached out to scratch Beaker.

"Who knows? The royals do lots of odd things. Ah, here it is."

Amelia watched for a few minutes. It was boring, really, mostly clips of Queen Elizabeth cutting ribbons, greeting famous people and riding in her carriage.

"I think I'm a closet royalist," Diane said, reaching into a bag of tortilla chips.

"Well, I'm not." One of Roshni's favorite topics was Kate and William. Why was it such a big deal?

She grabbed a handful of chips and got up to go. The image on the TV screen changed to a much younger-looking queen walking on her estate, surrounded by funny little brown dogs on leashes. Amelia counted eight of them.

The commentator called them Welsh corgis, which she had never heard of, and he talked about how much the queen loved her dogs. All in all, she'd owned more than thirty corgis, but she had only two left now, Willow and Holly. They had their own corgi room, where they slept in wicker baskets (raised to keep them out of drafts); their daily menu was posted on the kitchen wall (chuck steak, poached chicken, liver or rabbit), and when the queen traveled to one of her other castles, she always took her dogs along.

That was the end of the show. "Rats," Diane said. "I missed most of it. I really do *like* the queen. She has such a sense of duty. And she's so generous. I read in a magazine that she supports over six hundred charities."

"She does?"

"Apparently." Diane stood up and stretched. "Come on, Beaker. Let's go have your shower."

"Mom?"

"Yes?"

"Can I use the laptop? Just for a few minutes. Please?"

"Okay. But stay away from anything nasty. And I don't want you in your bedroom. Take it in the kitchen."

Amelia sighed. "When are you going to trust me?"

✵　✵　✵

She set up the laptop on the kitchen table. She found exactly what she was looking for on wikiHow.

How to Write to HM Queen Elizabeth II

She read the steps listed eagerly. It was pretty easy, really.

Address the Queen properly. "Your Majesty" is the preferred term.

If you refer to the Queen again in the letter, call her "Ma'am."

Amelia hesitated at the last step. *If you are a citizen of the United Kingdom, end the letter with "I have the honour to be, Madam, Your Majesty's humble and obedient subject." Otherwise, write "Respectfully yours" or "Faithfully yours."*

She darted down the hall and stuck her head in the bathroom door. Beaker was standing in the tub, and Diane was spraying him gently with the handheld showerhead.

"Beaker! Beaker! Beaker!" he said when he saw Amelia. He flapped his wings.

"Does he like that?" she said.

"Absolutely. He thinks he's in a tropical rainforest."

"Mom? Is Canada part of the United Kingdom?"

"Amelia! I can't believe you're going into grade seven and have to ask that! Of course not!"

Amelia sped back to the kitchen.

She scanned the site to see if she had missed anything important. *Make sure your penmanship is exquisite; otherwise, it is a good idea to type it.* No-brainer on that one. She hooked the laptop to the printer and got to work.

Your Majesty,

I have always thought Welsh corgis are the smartest, cutest and BEST dogs in the world. Even better than golden retrievers, which are my second favorite. Now I would like to tell you about some animals that need your help.

1. Mary is a crested gecko who escaped from her cage and hid under a couch. Her tail dropped off, and it won't grow back.

2. Zak is a Dumbo rat who has lung scarring and needs medicine every day.

3. Georgia is a Holland Lop bunny with epilepsy.

4. The Secretary is a ferret who has an eye infection. The other ferrets, The President and The Accountant, are too thin.

5. Romeo and Juliet are two turtles whose only crime was getting too big.

6. Apollo is a bearded dragon who was shut in a dark closet and has a bone disease.

7. Kilo is a Chinese water dragon who almost starved to death.

8. Beaker is a cockatiel who was burned under a hot tub.

9. Winston is a sulcata tortoise (who loves strawberries) who was left to die in a drainage ditch. He <u>might</u> get a disease, but we don't know yet.

There are lots more animals, and they all have sad stories. Would you like to help them, ma'am? You could join fifteen other celebrities (they have all been sent letters) in this worthy cause. Please look at the Duke's Den website (dukesden.com) for more information. Duke and Gabriella are the kindest people I know.

Faithfully yours,
Amelia Jacobs
P.S. Duke says that none of these animals asked to be here.

✤ ✤ ✤

The next morning, Amelia bolted her breakfast. "I'll be back in an hour!" she shouted. She sped out the front door before Diane could say no and half-walked, half-ran the six blocks to the post office, clutching her letter.

"I need this to go superfast," she said to the woman at the counter.

"Where is it going?" The woman was sorting booklets of stamps and didn't look up.

"Buckingham Palace."

"Buckingham Palace in London?"

"Yeah."

"Let me see."

Amelia handed her the envelope and waited.

"Is this a real address?"

"Yes."

The woman turned it over. Her lips twitched. Amelia had printed *URGENT* and *OPEN NOW!!!!!* on the back. She'd also drawn a picture of Winston with a talking balloon saying, *SAVE THE ANIMALS!!!* She'd figured it was a way to get Queen Elizabeth's attention.

Now she was suddenly unsure. "Is it okay to do that? It's not illegal or anything to write stuff on the envelope?"

"No, that's fine. Okay. You could send this Xpresspost-International. Three to four days guaranteed."

"Perfect," Amelia said.

"It'll cost $59.28."

"What? Are you joking? I don't have nearly that much!"

"Regular airmail then—$1.94. Up to seven business days."

"Business days! What does that mean? The weekend doesn't count?"

"Nope."

The woman didn't have to sound so cheerful. Amelia paid the money and watched her slap a stamp on her letter and drop it in a wire basket.

"It's not a busy time of year for mail. Not like Christmas. There's a good chance it will be there by next Friday."

"Great." Amelia sighed. Friday was a whole week away. Forever.

TWENTY-TWO

"You can't just run out the door without telling me where you're going," Diane said.

"Sorry." Amelia stared at her mother. Diane's face was covered in pale-green gunk. "What *is* that?"

"Avocado face mask."

"Oh. Yummy."

"I saved twenty dollars with those coupons Gabriella gave me. She seems a bit flighty, but I have to say she's thoughtful." Diane reached for her wallet on the kitchen counter and pulled out a ten-dollar bill. "I'll split the savings with Gabriella. She can buy a bag of lizard food or something."

"That's great, Mom. Can I give it to her now?"

"Okay. And Amelia?"

"What?"

"Dad called last night after you went to bed. He and his new…well, the rest of them are going camping on Salt Spring Island next weekend. He'd like you to come."

"He's taking a baby camping? That's dumb."

Diane grinned. "You said it. Not me."

Amelia sighed. "He probably just wants a babysitter."

Diane gave Amelia a hug. "Your dad loves you, sweetie. He's just not showing it very well right now. And it might be fun."

Amelia wriggled away. "I'll decide later."

✧ ✧ ✧

"*Parfait!*" Gabriella said.

"Par-faaay," Amelia repeated.

"*Magnifique!*"

"Mag-nee-feek!"

"*Fantastique!*"

"Fan-tas-teek!"

Gabriella was pulling soapy dishes out of the sink and stacking them haphazardly in the rack, and Amelia was drying.

"Your accent is improving," Gabriella said. "Pretty soon people will think you were born in Paris like me. And now we are finished. How about we look for some more coupons for your mother? I have found a new site on the Internet. And oh, I almost forgot. We have two new guests. They're in the living room."

The new arrivals were a pair of tiny toads, each one no bigger than Amelia's pinkie finger. They had dull green mottled backs and brilliant red bellies with black spots.

"They are called oriental fire-bellied toads," Gabriella said.

"They're amazing," Amelia said. When she had tired of watching the toads, she said, "Can Roshni come over for a while tonight?"

"Of course. Duke is working at the gas station—his first night!—so we will have a girls-only party. I will give you facials!" Gabriella gazed at the screen. "Is your mother still on her diet?"

"Who knows," Amelia said.

"*Save $5.00 when you buy two boxes of Splenda No-Calorie Sweetener.* We'll give it to her just in case." Gabriella clicked the mouse and sat back while the printer whirred. She looked at Amelia, her brown eyes, rimmed with black mascara, wide with hope. "The plan with Beaker is working? Your mom is changing her mind a teeny-tiny bit about making us go?"

Amelia thought about the envelope with the phone number for the house in Langley, hidden under her beanbag chair. "Not yet."

"July 23. That is not very far away. I've counted on the calendar. Only twenty-seven days to find a new place. And nobody wants our animals. What are we going to do?"

✵ ✵ ✵

Amelia and Roshni sat on the saggy couch, their feet propped up on the coffee table. Pale-green cucumber slices rested on their eyes. It had all felt *fantastique*—the gritty stuff called exfoliator that Gabriella said would help with blackheads, the goopy mask that tightened like cement and left their cheeks glowing, the silky moisturizing cream. Even better, Gabriella had promised that they could try some of her mascara and eye shadow when they were finished.

"I will be back in a few minutes," Gabriella said, her arms full of wet T-shirts. "I am going to hang these on the line."

"Are we going to tell her we wrote to the celebs?" Roshni whispered when Gabriella had gone.

"No," Amelia said. "It's a surprise."

She adjusted a slice of cucumber that was sliding down her cheek. She opened her mouth to tell Roshni about her letter to Queen Elizabeth and then changed her mind.

That was going to be the best surprise of all.

TWENTY-THREE

"The recipe's on the back of the Splenda box," Diane said. "Fifty calories per brownie. I've made two batches. Try one."

Amelia bit into a still-warm brownie. "You used the coupon already?"

"I whipped up to Safeway while you were having your facial. I saved sixteen dollars on the Splenda and Tide and toothpaste. And guess who was in the line behind me?"

"Who?"

"Our next-door neighbor."

"You mean Miss Snobby?" Amelia poked her finger through the bars of Beaker's cage and said, "Hey, Beaker," but he was nibbling on a spinach leaf and ignored her.

"She's not snobby at all," Diane said. "And her name is Marguerite. I think she's shy. We had a nice little chat about her flowers, and she's going to come over for iced tea tomorrow. I'll give her some brownies. She was *very* impressed with my coupons."

"Mom? The sixteen dollars you saved? Can half go to Gabriella and Duke?"

"Oh," Diane said. "Well, okay. That's fair. You can give them some brownies too. I don't want you going back down there tonight though. Wait till morning. And before you go to bed, wash all that stuff off your eyes. It'll stain your pillow."

Her mom was being very cool about the makeup, Amelia decided as she grabbed another brownie. Very un-Mom. Maybe some of Gabriella's style was rubbing off.

✷ ✷ ✷

"What on earth?" Diane said, staring out the kitchen window.

Amelia was supervising her strawberry Pop-Tart in the toaster (on weekends breakfast was anything goes), and it took her a few seconds to get to the window.

At least a dozen T-shirts lined the clothesline in the backyard, each one so riddled with holes that it looked like it was made out of lace. Tattered, falling-apart, almost-see-through lace.

"Are those Duke's?" Diane said. "It looks like someone's been using him for target practice."

"They're bedding for Zak and Lysander and the ferrets. They like to chew them."

"Marguerite must be having a fit having to look at that. It's an eyesore. Tell Gabriella she'll have to finish drying them inside. And don't forget I want you to meet Marguerite. She's coming at three."

✵ ✵ ✵

Amelia put six brownies on a plate and grabbed the four toonies that her mother had left for Gabriella. But when she got to the apartment door, she slammed to a halt. She could hear Gabriella's voice, shrill and angry, through the open kitchen window.

"You are crazy! Crazy! You borrow money from someone you do not even know? *C'est insupportable!* What are you thinking?"

"I know him now," Duke said. "We worked together all night. He's a good guy. I can tell."

"So? You tell him we are broke while you are pumping gas? You are begging now? What will he think of us?"

"He doesn't think anything. I told you, he's a good guy. We just started talking, and somehow it came up that I didn't have quite enough for the rent. I wasn't *begging*. And he said he could lend me some."

"How much?"

"Two hundred bucks."

Amelia heard Gabriella's breath come out in a whoosh. She felt like a spy, but she was frozen to the spot.

"Domenico said we can pay it back in a few weeks. It's not a big deal."

"Domenico? *Domenico?* What is his last name?"

"Something like Bellizi. Or maybe Bellizo. I don't remember."

"*Mon dieu!* He is Italian!"

"So? What does that mean?"

"It means that he could belong to the Mafia! Have you never heard of the Mafia shooting people's knees when they do not pay them back?"

Amelia felt cold with shock. But Duke burst into laughter. "That is the stupidest thing I've ever heard. Not to mention totally bigoted. I'm going out."

The door flung open before Amelia could flee. Her cheeks flamed, but Duke just gave her a friendly grin.

"Hey," he said. "Just what I ordered."

He grabbed the biggest brownie and disappeared.

* * *

"The Mafia!" Roshni squealed. "That is seriously scary!"

"I know." Amelia took a slurp of her Blizzard and watched Liam approach their booth, balancing fries, onion rings, a cheeseburger and a giant Coke.

"God, Liam," Roshni said. "It's not even eleven o' clock. Is that supposed to be breakfast?"

"Hey," Liam said, "Dad's treating." Liam's dad had given him twenty-five bucks and told him to take his friends to Dairy Queen to celebrate the end of school.

Twenty-five bucks, and it wasn't even his birthday. Amelia thought it would have been better to put it in

Gabriella's pickle jar. Gabriella kept the jar on the kitchen counter, with random change in it, and had dropped the ten-dollar bill from the day before into it as well as the toonies Amelia had given her that morning.

"Is there any change?" Amelia said, thinking of the jar.

"Not much. You girls are expensive dates."

This is such a waste of good money, Amelia thought glumly as she sucked up the last of her Blizzard.

"Dates?" Roshni said. "You wish."

TWENTY-FOUR

When Amelia got home from Dairy Queen, Simon's van was parked out front. Duke came around the corner of the house. "Hey, Amelia. Want to come? We're going to pick up a bird."

"Okay!" Amelia dashed inside to tell her mom and then scrambled into the backseat.

"How far are we going?" she said.

"Just across the bridge to North Vancouver. It's a house at the top of Lonsdale Avenue. Simon knows where it is."

Amelia was full of questions about the bird, but Duke tilted his seat back and said, "I didn't get home from the gas station until six this morning. I'm gonna get some sleep."

Simon didn't want to talk either. He grunted a greeting to Amelia, yelled at the driver in the car ahead of him to learn how to drive, and then said, "It's time for *Quirks & Quarks*" and turned on the radio.

✵ ✵ ✵

"This is Upside-Down Mango," said the man, who introduced himself as Perry. "He used to like hanging upside down from the bars in his cage. But he doesn't want to do anything now. He just sits there."

Perry had brought Amelia and Duke into a large, very clean kitchen with copper pots hanging from the ceiling, and an enormous island with a marble top. A birdcage sat on the island, and on the bottom of the cage, in the corner, a little bird huddled. He was a bright mossy green, with a red head, a red-and-peach bib and brilliant blue tail feathers.

"He's gorgeous!" Amelia said.

"He's a lovebird," Perry said. "He's pretty, I'll give you that. He was my wife's, and she passed away and now I'm stuck with him."

He sighed. "Is it possible for a bird to go into shock?"

"Definitely," Duke said. "Tell me exactly what happened."

"It's going to sound pretty funny, but here's the story. My wife spoiled Mango like crazy and let him ride around on her shoulder all day long, so now, if I leave him in his cage, he has temper tantrums and rattles the bars. When I can't stand it any longer, I let him out. And I let him out yesterday morning and he flew into a chocolate pudding!"

"What?" Duke said.

"A hot chocolate pudding. I like to cook, and I had just taken the pudding off the stove. It was boiling hot and still bubbling, and I admit, I had kind of forgotten about Mango.

He landed with this splash right in the middle of it." Perry grinned. "I told you it would sound kind of funny."

"Actually, it doesn't sound funny at all," Duke said. "So what did you do?"

"Well, I stuck him under the tap to cool him down and washed all the pudding off and put him back in his cage. He hasn't moved since, but he's alive. You can see him breathing."

Duke opened the cage and gently picked up the little bird. Amelia held her breath while he examined him. "He's in shock for sure," he said finally. "Most of his toenails have fallen off, but I think he'll get better."

"His toenails? Really? Well, he did land feet first." Perry chuckled, and Amelia felt a flash of anger.

"He never bit Sandra, but I can't stop him from biting me, and I'd been meaning to call you even before this happened. Someone gave me your website name, and I know you mostly take reptiles and probably don't want him—"

"I want him," Duke said.

✵ ✵ ✵

Diane and Marguerite were sitting on lawn chairs in the front yard, with glasses of iced tea and a plate of brownies, when the van pulled up. Duke had tucked Mango under his T-shirt, and the little bird had ridden home resting on Duke's chest. Duke said he could feel Mango's tiny heart, which was beating way too fast, start to slow down.

Duke put Mango back in his cage and lifted it out of the van, and Amelia carried a bag of birdseed. "Thanks, Si," Duke said, and Simon sped away, waving one arm out the window.

Diane called out, "What have you got now?"

"It's a lovebird," Amelia said. "Come and see."

Diane and Marguerite walked over and peered into the cage.

"Oh my, he's beautiful," Marguerite said. "He looks like a miniature parrot."

"He is a parrot," Duke said.

"He doesn't look very happy," Diane said.

"His name is Upside-Down Mango," Amelia said. "He fell into a pot of boiling chocolate pudding, and his toenails got burned off."

Diane looked horrified. "That's terrible!"

"Can he live without his toenails?" Marguerite asked.

"They'll probably mostly grow back," Duke said. "But he won't be able to cling to any of his perches for a while."

"I haven't even introduced you," Diane said. "This is my daughter, Amelia, and Duke, who lives downstairs and has all the animals I told you about. This is our neighbor, Marguerite."

"Hi," Duke and Amelia said at the same time.

"Hello," Marguerite said. "I've seen you go by, Amelia, but you always seem in a rush."

"What are you going to do with that poor little thing?" Diane said.

"Keep him warm. And unstressed. He's been traumatized. And I think he's been neglected for a long time.

He needs some pampering. Lovebirds are social and bond with people pretty easily. He'll come around. Right now, I better take him inside and get him settled."

"I've got a much more sensible idea," Diane said. "Mango, how would you like to come and live with me?"

TWENTY-FIVE

"**B**eaker will be a good influence," Diane said. "He's been through a great deal himself."

Duke had put Mango's cage close to Beaker's. "Beaker! Beaker! Beaker!" Beaker called out. He hopped to a higher perch and wagged his tail.

"I've never seen that before," Marguerite said. "Just like a dog!" She had just rinsed the iced-tea glasses under the tap and put the plastic wrap back on the brownies. She wasn't snobby at all, Amelia thought.

"I wouldn't let them out at the same time," Duke said. "Not yet anyway. We'll give Mango some fresh water and some of Beaker's pellets, and then we'll just let him get used to things. And I'll throw that bag of birdseed away. It's meant for wild songbirds. Perry probably got it on sale or something."

"Mango's watching Beaker," Amelia said. "Do you think he knows Beaker's another kind of bird?"

"A bald bird?" Duke said, grinning.

Beaker gave a piercing screech. "Really, Duke," Diane said indignantly.

"Sorry, Beaker," Duke said. "No offense intended."

✻ ✻ ✻

Duke came up to check on Mango after supper. Gabriella came too, so she could meet the new arrival. "My aunt has a lovebird. In Paris. They have so much personality. You will enjoy him, Diane, when he feels like himself."

"I'm enjoying him now," Diane said. "He and Beaker have been having quite a conversation. They're very funny."

After Duke and Gabriella left, Amelia spotted an envelope on the end of the counter. She picked it up and opened it.

"What is it?" Diane said.

Amelia pulled out a check. "I think it's the rent."

"Let me see." Diane studied the check. "It *is* the rent. It's a few days early." She sounded confused.

"You have to admit, Duke and Gabriella are reliable," Amelia said.

"Yes, they are."

"Does that mean—?"

"It doesn't mean anything," Diane said.

✻ ✻ ✻

Just before bed, Amelia sat down at the end of the living-room couch and dialed her father's number. She planned to keep the phone call short and to the point.

"I can't go," she blurted out when her dad answered.

"What? Who is this—Amelia? Is that you?"

Amelia had rehearsed her excuse. "I can't go camping with you on Salt Spring Island because I'm helping look after our tenants' animals, and they need me. I'm really really sorry, but—"

A baby screamed in the background, which made Amelia jump. "Christ!" her dad said. She heard him yell, "Can't you do something?" and then he said, "You never screamed when you were teething, Amelia. Never! You were a perfect baby. Hang on for a sec."

Amelia set the phone down gently. She went to find her mother, who was in bed with a cup of tea in one hand and an open textbook in the other.

Amelia burst into tears.

✿ ✿ ✿

"No talking," Diane said. "You're going to let yourself float away. That's what a great massage is all about. Total relaxation."

Amelia wriggled on her tummy until her face was lined up with the hole in the massage table.

"Ready?" Diane said.

"Ready." She felt her mother's hands press into her shoulders. A delicious pineapple scent filled the air. For a few minutes she watched her mother's bare feet through the hole, and then she closed her eyes.

"Comfy?" Diane said.

"Mmm." Amelia was surprised how strong her mother's hands were. Strong and gentle at the same time.

Floating away. That's exactly what it felt like. She was on a fluffy white cloud, sipping pineapple juice and drifting through the blue sky.

TWENTY-SIX

"You get to name this one," Duke said. He cradled a small brown lizard in his hands. "It's an armadillo lizard."

The lizard had hard, spiny scales from the top of its head to the tip of its tail. "Can I hold it?" Amelia said.

Duke slipped the lizard into her hands. It curled up, sticking the end of its tail right into its mouth and forming a small prickly ball.

"He's scared," Duke said. "That's why he's doing that. To protect himself. Let's put him back in his tank."

Amelia set the little lizard gently onto a bed of soft dirt.

"He's emaciated," Duke said. "He was probably wild-caught. There's a trade from Africa. They get packed in plastic bins by the thousands and shipped here through Mexico."

"That's so horrible."

"Thought of a name yet?"

She looked at the tiny spiny lizard. "Pinecone."

✵ ✵ ✵

"Well?" Roshni said. "Anything?"

"Nothing." Amelia had run upstairs when she heard the mailman's whistle on the front sidewalk, even though she knew it was way too soon.

"What's taking them so long?" Roshni lifted Georgia out of her cage and plunked down on the couch.

"It's Wednesday," Liam said. "We mailed the letters last Thursday. That's, like, six days ago."

"Thank you, Liam. I can count."

"Besides—"

"We know," Amelia said. "You think they won't send money. But Roshni and I think they will."

Liam shrugged. "I'm going to go hang out with the snakes."

Duke and Gabriella had gone out, and Amelia was in charge. She had asked Liam and Roshni to hold the turtles Romeo and Juliet while she dumped buckets of dirty water from their bin into the bathtub. When the bin was almost empty, she dragged it to the bathroom and tipped it into the tub to pour out the last bit of water. Then she dragged it back to the hallway and filled it with buckets of clean, cool tap water.

Then she'd run up to check the mail, and now she was back. She thought of one more thing to do. She went into the kitchen and got Mary's gecko food out of the fridge. She mixed the food carefully in a little dish—two table-spoons of a brownish powder that smelled like fruit and one tablespoon of water. She covered it with plastic wrap and put it in the fridge to sit for a while.

She spotted the last of the strawberries in a saucer behind a bowl of mac and cheese. She cut one up for Winston and took it into the reptile room.

Liam was sitting on the floor beside King Kong's tank. "I am so not going to miss the next time Duke feeds him. I can't believe you didn't call me."

"Get over it." Amelia crouched down and dropped the pieces of strawberry into Winston's pen.

The tortoise didn't move from his corner. He didn't even turn his head.

"Hey, Winston," Amelia said, surprised. She picked up a piece of strawberry and dropped it right beside his front foot. Winston stared straight ahead.

Her surprise turned to icy fear. "Oh my god! Winston's sick!"

✻ ✻ ✻

"We don't need to panic," Duke said. "Maybe he's just tired."

But Amelia could tell he was worried. She had called him on his cell, and he'd come home right away. Amelia, Duke, Liam and Roshni were crowded around Winston's pen, staring at the tortoise.

"Could it be that disease from being in the drainage ditch?" Amelia said.

"Not a disease. A respiratory infection," Duke said. "It's called Runny Nose Syndrome."

Amelia squatted down and examined Winston's tiny nostrils. "There's nothing coming out of his nose."

"That's good. But it's weird he doesn't want to eat."

"It said on the Internet that a sulcata tortoise is an eating machine."

Duke smiled. "That's true."

"So that makes it even worse that he's not eating, right?"

"Runny Nose Syndrome," Roshni said. "Is that kind of like a cold in humans?"

"Not exactly. It's more serious than that. It can lead to pneumonia and even renal failure."

"But we don't know he has it," Amelia said quickly.

"No, we don't." Duke stood up. "Too many people in here. That's going to stress him out even more. Let's leave him alone for a while."

Amelia took one last look at Winston as they filed out the door. "Promise you'll come and get me if anything happens."

"Promise," Duke said.

TWENTY-SEVEN

I n the afternoon, Duke took the bus to Coquitlam to look at a snake. Amelia used Gabriella's laptop to hunt for coupons.

Gabriella was on her phone. It sounded like she was talking to different salons, because she kept saying, "I could drop off a résumé." Every call ended with her sighing and saying, "Well, thanks anyway," and then muttering, "*Merde*" as she punched in another number.

Amelia walked past Gabriella to get some juice and noticed two rows of phone numbers on the paper, one for beauty salons, she figured, and the other with the word *Apartment?* scribbled at the top. Her stomach tightened.

She went back to the laptop and sorted her coupons into two piles.

The pile for her mom had coupons for Royale bathroom tissue, Yoplait yogurt, Sunlight dish detergent, Betty Crocker chocolate cake mix, Domino's Pizza, Häagen-Dazs ice cream.

Gabriella's had ones for L'Oréal lip gloss, Maybelline mascara, Cover Girl blush.

"Check Walmart," Gabriella said between phone calls. "They have good deals."

They did. Eyeliner for Gabriella and Old El Paso salsa for her mom. There were gardening coupons, too, for a tub of something called Miracle-Gro and a watering can Amelia thought Marguerite might like. She printed them off and clipped them.

When Duke got back, he and Amelia tried to coax Winston to eat some canned pumpkin.

"He's just not hungry," she said, disappointed. "What should we do?"

"Nothing right now." Duke squatted beside Winston's pen. "Hey, old buddy, what's wrong?"

"I wish animals could talk to us," Amelia said.

"They can. We just have to learn how to listen."

✴ ✴ ✴

In the morning Amelia skipped breakfast and rushed down to the apartment. Duke was standing in the kitchen, spreading peanut butter on a piece of toast, and Gabriella was putting on her makeup in the bathroom. The door was open, and she called, "Hey, Amelia. We were just going to get you. Do you want something to eat?"

"Not now." She couldn't eat, not until she had seen Winston. "How is he?"

"Not great," Duke said. "The tissue around his eyes is puffed up, and he's wheezing a bit. And there's stuff bubbling out of his nostrils. I've phoned Simon. He's bringing the van over so we can take him to the vet."

"I'm coming with you."

✹ ✹ ✹

Amelia sat in the backseat, beside the cardboard box carrying Winston. Duke had draped a towel over the box, but she hoped Winston would know she was right beside him. She thought Simon veered around corners way too fast and that Winston might get scared.

The best vet for reptiles was in Burnaby. Simon listened to the directions and then said, "Yo, bro, let's go."

Simon said he knew a few shortcuts. Amelia waited for him to yell at a black car in front of them that dawdled at an intersection, but Simon was silent. He's worried about Winston too, she thought.

When they got to the vet's office, Duke said, "I'd rather take him in by myself. Too many people is confusing."

Simon held the van door open, and Duke lifted the box out. A man with a gray poodle on a leash came out of the vet's office, and Duke and Winston disappeared inside.

Amelia wanted to stay right there in the van and not budge, but Simon said, "We passed a McDonald's just back there. How about an Egg McMuffin?"

She started to say no, but then changed her mind. She was a tiny bit hungry, after all, and McDonald's was fast.

TWENTY-EIGHT

"Is it Runny Nose Syndrome?" Amelia asked.

"It looks like it," Duke said. "The vet took a culture, so we'll know more later. But we're going to treat it like it's a respiratory infection. He's given me some tetracycline."

Duke had put Winston's box back on the seat beside Amelia, and she could hear the tortoise wheezing, right through the towel. "What's tetracycline?"

"An antibiotic." Duke turned and smiled at Amelia. "He's going to be okay."

"Is it a pill? How are you going to make him take it?"

"It's liquid. I'll squirt it in his nose with a syringe. The vet gave him his first dose right now, and he doesn't get any more until Sunday. He only gets it every three days."

Every three days? How was that going to work? "Can't you give it to him more often? Just in case."

"Tortoises have a slow metabolism. They're not like people. It's pretty effective, Amelia. He'll get better."

"What if he doesn't?"

"There's another, stronger drug. The vet's ordering some in just in case we need it. But it'll take a while to get."

"How long?"

"At least a couple of weeks. It's not something vets normally carry because it's so expensive."

Amelia stared out the window. She wished Winston could have the stronger drug right away.

Simon drummed his fingers while the SUV in front of them decided whether to go through the intersection or turn left. The light went red, and Simon sighed.

"How much so far?" he said to Duke.

"Seventy-five bucks for the culture and a hundred bucks for the antibiotic and forty-five bucks for the consultation."

Simon whistled softly. "That other drug?"

"You don't want to know."

When they got home, Amelia took Duke's book about bearded dragons into the reptile room and settled beside Winston's pen. After half an hour, sweat was trickling down her neck. She tiptoed when she left the room. Winston wasn't wheezing anymore, which was a hopeful sign, and she thought he might be asleep.

✸ ✸ ✸

"Check out this watering can!" Marguerite called over the fence the next morning. "It's a dandy! It has an extra-long spout, so I can reach my hanging baskets."

Amelia thought it was totally weird to get so excited about a watering can, but she liked Marguerite. Marguerite popped in almost every day with leafy treats from her garden for Beaker and Mango, and Amelia had taken her down to the apartment to meet all the animals. She hung over the fence now and watched Marguerite water a bed of tall purple flowers. "Your garden is looking amazing."

"Thank you. And how is Winston doing? Is he eating again?"

"He's got Runny Nose Syndrome. We took him to the vet yesterday. He's on antibiotics. It was mega expensive."

"I almost forgot. Hang on a sec." Marguerite disappeared inside and came out with a ten-dollar bill. "Half of my savings on the watering can. You can give that to Gabriella and Duke. Every little bit helps."

"That's what Mom does! She gives them half of what she saves with the coupons. We're putting it in a pickle jar."

"That's where I got the idea. From your mom."

✿ ✿ ✿

Amelia and Gabriella spent the morning hunting for coupons.

"It's too bad we don't know someone who has a cat," Gabriella said. "Or someone who has a baby. There are always so many coupons for cat stuff and baby stuff."

"I know someone with seven cats," Amelia said. "And I know someone with triplets. Well, I sort of know them." She peered over Gabriella's shoulder.

At the top of the screen there were coupons for Purina Friskies cat food, Temptations cat treats and clumping cat litter. Gabriella scrolled down to the baby section: Huggies diapers, baby wipes and Heinz baby-food pouches.

"Can I print these?" Amelia said.

When she left the apartment, her head was whirring with excitement. She was going to ask Liam and Roshni to go with her. No way did she have the guts to go by herself.

TWENTY-NINE

"Have you even met this dude?" Liam said.

"No," Amelia said. "But I've seen him in the window. And he must be nice if he owns that many cats."

In the end, just Liam had come along because Roshni was finally getting her hair streaked. It was her birthday present from a month and a half ago, and she'd been saving it while she agonized over what color to get.

The guy with the holey jeans and the lip stud was in his driveway, polishing the Mustang, when Liam and Amelia walked past.

"Drool away," he yelled, and Liam hollered back, "Where did you get it? A scrapyard?"

Then they were in front of the cat house, only today there were no cats. "They must be inside," Amelia said.

"Are you sure this is the right house?" Liam asked.

"Come on."

She clutched the coupons with one hand and rang the doorbell with the other. The door opened so quickly that they both leaped back.

"You're selling chocolate bars, right?" said the biggest, blackest man Amelia had ever seen. He was wearing gray sweatpants and a gray sweatshirt with the sleeves cut off. He grinned. "For the Scouts."

Amelia's heart felt like it was pounding in her ears. "Not exactly. I mean, *no*."

"I was just kidding." The man leaned against the door-jamb while Amelia told him, her voice shaking, all about Duke's Den and how she was trying to raise money by finding coupons for people.

She was nearing the end of her speech when a kitchen timer rang, and he said, "Back in a sec" and disappeared down a hallway.

"That is one seriously built guy," Liam whispered. "He's got muscles on top of muscles."

Amelia wasn't listening. She was kneeling down and stroking a gray cat and a black-and-white cat that were winding themselves around her legs.

Then the man was back. "Banana bread's done," he said. "That's Mr. Mistoffelees and Skimbleshanks."

"Cool names." Amelia gave the gray cat one last pat and stood up.

"I got them from T.S. Eliot. He's this poet who wrote a book about cats. My other cats are called Bustopher Jones, Rum Tum Tugger, Macavity, Mungojerrie and Rumpleteazer."

"That's amazing," Amelia said.

"Now let me get this straight. You want me to take these coupons and give you half the money I save to help a sick tortoise?"

"That's about it," Liam said.

"This is for real?"

Amelia nodded.

"How do I know you're legit?"

"Um…"

"Just kidding. Okay, why not? You look like nice kids."

"Really?" Amelia said.

"Sure."

"*Thank* you."

"Do you pump iron by any chance, dude?" Liam said. "Or play football?"

"I'm a personal trainer. I'm Jordan, by the way."

"I'm Amelia."

"I'm Liam."

"That's settled then," Jordan said.

"Well, thanks again." Amelia handed Jordan the coupons. "We'll come back in a few days."

"Hey, Liam," Jordan said. "Why don't you come down to the gym, and I'll get you started with something easy? Twenty-pounders."

"Uh…" Liam stammered.

"Just kidding." Jordan scooped up a tortoiseshell cat and closed the door.

✢　✢　✢

"Now what?" said Liam. "How are we going to find the triplets lady?"

"Good question." Amelia had seen the woman with the stroller six times now, but she had never seen her come out of a house or driveway. She usually went right past their house to the chain-link fence and then back again. So Amelia figured she had to live somewhere in the neighborhood. But where?

It was too hot to keep walking up and down the street, so they parked themselves in Amelia's front yard. She went inside and brought out two cans of Coke.

"This is very boring," Liam said when he had drained his can and squished it flat. "And pointless. We could be here all day hoping she'll go by. Why don't you come over to my house and we can play some games?"

Amelia thought computer games were boring too, but Duke was out and Gabriella finally had a day at the salon, so there was nothing else to do.

"Okay. But I'll bring the coupons with me. Just in case."

THIRTY

On Sunday, Amelia watched Duke slowly push the end of the plastic syringe, dripping the antibiotic into Winston's tiny nostrils. When he was finished, he filled another syringe with water and squirted it into the tortoise's mouth.

"He was nibbling his hay today," Amelia said. "That's good, isn't it?"

"Very good. We just gotta make sure he doesn't get dehydrated. And I'm going to set up another heat lamp for him."

"He's getting better, right? The tetracycline stuff is working. We probably won't even need that other expensive drug."

✯   ✯   ✯

"I can't believe your mom let you do that," Amelia said.

Roshni was staying overnight at her house. Diane had let her in, and Roshni had surprised Amelia in her bedroom with a loud *Ta-da!*

"Do you *love* it?" Roshni said.

Amelia stared at the wild turquoise and pink streaks in Roshni's black hair. She opened her mouth to say something and then changed her mind and closed it.

"Well?"

"It's different."

Roshni seemed satisfied with that. "I know. You should ask for streaks too. For your birthday. No offense, but you need a bit of jazzing up."

"Thanks a lot."

"When exactly is your birthday anyway? Are you having a party?"

"July 22. And who would I invite? You and Liam? Three whole people. That would be a lot of fun. In case you haven't noticed, I don't exactly know anyone else around here."

"Yeesh. Calm down. Fire-engine red. Your streaks. I dare you."

※ ※ ※

Amelia and Roshni spent the next half hour trying to get Mango to say, "I'm a pretty boy" (wasn't he supposed to be a parrot?) and then went downstairs to check on Winston.

Usually the apartment door was open, but this time it was shut, and when Amelia knocked, no one answered.

"They must be out." She stood on tiptoe and peered in the window of the reptile room, but the curtain was pulled and all she could make out was Bill's cranky eye glaring back at her through the crack.

"Let's go make some popcorn," Roshni said.

"Okay."

But when Amelia and Roshni turned around the side of the house, they came to a sudden stop. A motorcycle was idling on the street at the end of the walk, and a guy with a thin ponytail, dressed in black leather, called out, "Is this where Duke lives?"

"Yeah," Amelia said. The guy had an accent, but he didn't sound like Gabriella. "In the basement apartment."

The guy turned off his motorcycle and climbed off. He was wearing cowboy boots, and several loops of chain hung from the sleeves of his leather coat. "The door is where?"

"Around there," Amelia said, pointing.

"But Duke's not home," Roshni added.

He frowned and walked past the girls, disappearing around the back.

"Wait a sec," Amelia said to Roshni. She followed him to the corner of the house, poking her head around cautiously, and then reported to Roshni, "He's looking in the windows!"

Then he was back, his chains swinging.

"*Ciao*," he said.

"*Ciao*," Roshni called as they watched him climb on the motorcycle and speed away. She turned to Amelia. "That's Italian for hello or goodbye."

"Italian?"

They stared at each other. "OH MY GOD!" they said at the same time.

* * *

"We just came this close to the Mafia," Roshni said.

"Maybe," Amelia said.

"Maybe? Black leather? Chains? And did you see his face when I said Duke wasn't home?"

"He was smiling when he came back."

"A sinister smile."

"I should have asked him if his name was Domenico," Amelia said.

"How many other Italians d'you think are looking for Duke? He's gotta be Domenico."

"What do you think he wanted?"

"The *money*, Amelia. Isn't that obvious? Gabriella's right. Duke was majorly dumb to borrow it." Roshni stood at the kitchen window, gazing out at the shadowy street. "Is your mom getting home soon?"

Was Roshni really that scared? Hard to tell. "She said ten thirty at the latest. She's practising her massage moves at Jeannie's."

Amelia counted the pops coming from the microwave. When it slowed to three, spaced far apart, she opened the door and took out the bag of popcorn.

"One good thing," Roshni said. "Domenico knows that Duke lives in the basement."

"Why is that good?" Amelia dumped the popcorn into a bowl and started picking out the burnt kernels.

"He won't come after *us* by mistake."

Amelia snorted. "He's gone, Roshni. Are you going to stay by that window all night?"

"Maybe—oh!"

"What?"

"There goes that triplets woman you've been looking for."

THIRTY-ONE

"**N**ow? It's almost dark." Amelia ran to the window. "I don't see her. Which way was she going?"

"That way." Roshni pointed to the end of the street. "She was going fast."

"Then she'll be coming back. Come on!" Amelia grabbed the baby coupons, which she had left beside the phone, and ran to the front door.

When she and Roshni got to the street, they heard screaming before they saw the stroller.

"God! Someone's being murdered," Roshni said.

"Let me do the talking," Amelia said as the woman and the stroller came into sight.

The woman was hunched over the stroller, her long hair hanging like a curtain over her face, and she let out a scream too when Amelia shouted, "Hi!"

"Sorry," the woman said, pushing her hair behind her ears. "I didn't see you standing there. It's getting kinda dark."

Amelia walked over and peered into the stroller at three round scarlet faces. The babies stopped screaming and stared at her with surprised looks.

"Are they teething?" she said.

"Yeah." The woman sighed. "Usually I stick them on top of the washing machine and the vibration makes them go to sleep, but tonight nothing is working."

"That's harsh," Roshni said.

"You're telling me."

"I'm Amelia," Amelia said. "I live in that house. And this is my friend Roshni."

"Strawberry," the woman said. "I know—weird name. It's because of my strawberry-blond hair."

Amelia thought Strawberry's hair was more like dirty blond. It looked greasy, as if she hadn't had time to wash it. There were black circles under Strawberry's eyes. Up close, she looked pretty young, almost like she could still be a teenager.

"Have you got a sec?" Amelia said.

When she was finished her story, Strawberry gazed at Amelia's house and said, "All those snakes and things are in there?"

"Yeah, but they won't hurt anyone."

"I don't know. Coupons? It just sounds like a lot of work."

"You could use the savings to pay for a babysitter," Roshni said.

"I don't know. I guess." Strawberry sighed. "I could try. But I'm not promising anything."

"Thanks," Amelia said. "And if you like these, I can get you lots more."

She and Roshni watched Strawberry push the stroller up the street.

"I'm never having kids," Roshni said.

"Me neither."

"And hey, how did *you* know about teething?"

Amelia sighed. "Dad."

✡ ✡ ✡

The next night, Gabriella invited Amelia and Diane for crepes. It was the first time Diane had been back to the apartment, and she looked surprised when she walked into the kitchen. Gabriella must have been cleaning for hours, Amelia thought. The counters were cleared off except for a large bowl of batter, and there were no dishes stacked in the sink.

"Please, sit down," Gabriella said. "We will eat very soon."

"Let me help instead," Diane said. "I actually own a crepe pan, but I've never attempted to make them."

"Then I will give you a lesson!" Gabriella said.

Amelia watched for a few minutes. It didn't look that hard. You just had to swirl the batter in the pan—and not put too much in—then flip the crepe over when it started to bubble. Crepes were just very skinny pancakes.

She thought her mother was overreacting when she took her first crepe out of the pan and shrieked, "I can't believe I did that!"

Gabriella declared, "*Parfait!*" and added it to a growing stack on a plate.

Amelia went into the living room. She said hi to Duke, who was on his laptop, and then wandered into the reptile room to check on Winston, who was sleeping.

"We are ready!" Gabriella cried.

They all crowded around the little table in the kitchen. Gabriella set a plate of crepes in the middle.

"*Bon appétit!*"

The best part about these crepes was the filling. Thick, rich chocolate sauce, sliced bananas and mounds of whipped cream, all rolled up inside the crepe. It was like having dessert for your main course. They were almost finished when Gabriella's phone rang.

"Yes," she said. "I am the one who called…July 23… Yes…Oh…Well, that is too bad, but we are definitely still interested…How about tomorrow night, if we can get a ride?"

"What's too bad?" Duke said when Gabriella put down her phone.

"The apartment on Craigslist. The one in Port Moody? It only has one bedroom."

Amelia had trouble swallowing. Diane put her fork down and stared at Gabriella. "How would you manage with one bedroom?" she said.

"We will give it to the reptiles. Duke and I will sleep on a couch in the living room, and we will keep our clothes in boxes."

"That's just ridiculous."

"We have done it before. Right, Duke? That place we had before with the—what do you call it?"

"Mildew," Duke mumbled through a mouthful of crepe.

Diane shuddered. "What happened with the house in Langley? Jeannie's niece's house?"

Gabriella looked blank.

"It's a long story," Amelia said. "I'll tell you later, Mom. Why don't you have the last crepe?"

Port Moody? That was as far away as Langley. She shoved her plate away. She couldn't eat another bite.

✳ ✳ ✳

"Turtle Wax," Amelia said. "I'm not kidding. That's what it says."

"Let me see." Gabriella leaned over her shoulder. "Buy one, get two free. That is a very good deal."

"Romeo and Juliet!" Amelia said. "I bet it would make their shells all shiny."

"But why do turtles want shiny shells?" Gabriella mused. "Ask Duke. If he says it is a good idea, we will print it."

Duke was outside, mowing the lawn. "Turtle Wax is for polishing cars," he said with a huge grin.

"It is?"

"Yup. Last time I looked, Romeo and Juliet didn't have any chrome."

"Not funny," Amelia said.

✮ ✮ ✮

"I must be crazy. That guy hates me," Liam said.

Roshni poked his arm. "Shut up and keep walking."

"Maybe he'll be outside polishing his car," Amelia said. "That'll make it easier."

But he wasn't. They walked cautiously around the gleaming Mustang and up to the front door of the house. Amelia rang the bell.

A woman in a pink housecoat opened the door.

"Uh, we wanted to talk to the owner of the red car," Amelia said.

The woman turned around and hollered, "Mick! Haul yourself outta bed! Someone to see you!"

She disappeared, and after what seemed like ages Mick appeared, yawning and wearing a pair of pyjama bottoms and a T-shirt.

He stared at them, and his face darkened. "Yeah?"

"I'm Amelia, and this is Liam and Roshni."

"So?"

"Not going well," Liam whispered.

Amelia glared at him and then launched into her story, which was punctuated by Mick's yawns.

"You got me outta bed for this?" he said when she stopped to take a breath. "A bunch of lizards and rats and a dumb tortoise? You must be crazy."

"That's what I said," Liam chipped in. "Crazy. Coming here, I mean…"

Mick gave him a penetrating look. Then he said, "Tell me again. What's in it for me?"

"Free Turtle Wax," Roshni said. "With only a small fee going to Duke's Den."

"Let me see." Mick grabbed the coupon from Amelia and squinted at it. "Yeah, okay, I'll do it."

"Great!" Amelia said. "Can I come back tomorrow for the money?"

"What's the big hurry? Come back in a few days. And not so early. I like to sleep in."

He turned to Liam. "And you, punk, don't even think—"

"Of breathing on your car," Liam finished.

"You got that right."

THIRTY-TWO

Amelia gave Winston his third dose of tetracycline. She bit down hard on her lower lip as she squeezed the drops of liquid into his tiny nostrils.

"You're good at that," Duke said. "You're really a great helper."

"Thanks. I'm going to stay in here for a while."

"Sounds good. I'll phone around some more. There's a vet out in the Valley I haven't tried."

Since the day before, Winston had been breathing with his mouth open. Gasping, more like it, Amelia thought. The bubbly stuff was back, oozing out of his nostrils. She felt sick with fear.

Duke had called the vet in Burnaby, who said he was having trouble getting the other drug. *Maybe in a couple of weeks*, he'd said.

We can't wait a couple of weeks, Duke had replied.

Someone *had* to have the drug somewhere. Duke had spent all morning calling vets. So far no luck.

Amelia walked around the room, peering into the cages and pens. Bill sprawled on his branch, watching her. The snakes were curled up in balls. Kilo floated in her pool. Apollo and Oliver were asleep.

No one is moving, she thought.

They're holding their breath too and praying for Winston.

✵ ✵ ✵

On Thursday morning Marguerite brought over some kale from her garden for Mango and Beaker, and a huge zucchini for Diane. Amelia watched her mom take the zucchini with a brave smile—it was their fourth in four days.

"It's a bumper crop," Marguerite announced happily as she accepted a cup of coffee from Diane. "I don't know why I've never planted them before. Who knew six plants would produce so much?"

"Who knew," Diane repeated. She poured herself a coffee too and sat at the table with Amelia and Marguerite.

"What are those?" Amelia asked as Marguerite spread half a dozen small pieces of colored cardboard, each one a different shade of beige, on the table.

"Paint chips. I'm painting my living room. I need some help deciding."

Amelia turned over each chip and read the name out loud. "Oyster, pearl, egg shell, bone white, mushroom."

"Are you doing it yourself?" Diane said.

"I'm getting that girl across the street. Rachel. She has a reno business. She left a card under my door. Great timing, because I'd just decided to paint."

"We got one of her cards too," Diane said. "Maybe next year."

"No offense," Amelia said, "but don't you think these colors are boring? Why don't you be original and paint your living room purple?"

Diane and Marguerite stared at her.

Amelia got up with her cereal bowl. "I *like* purple."

✯ ✯ ✯

Amelia went over to Marguerite's in the afternoon. She'd printed two coupons, one for weed killer and one for a seed-starter kit.

The door was open, and voices drifted from the living room.

"Come in," Marguerite shouted. "We're in here."

Marguerite and a girl in paint-spattered overalls were standing in the middle of the room. Amelia recognized her right away. Rachel, from Rachel's Renos across the street.

"Rachel, this is our neighbor Amelia," Marguerite said.

"Hi," Amelia said.

Rachel was chewing gum vigorously. She stopped chewing and grinned at Amelia. "I've seen you around. Hiya." She turned to Marguerite. "Awesome color. I get so sick of painting oyster walls. Purple. I love it!"

"Mauve," Marguerite said quickly. "Pale mauve. It was… well, Amelia's idea."

Rachel grinned at Amelia. "Very contemporary."

"Thanks."

"That wraps it up." Rachel blew a big pink bubble and popped it. "I got all the measurements I need. D'you want me to wait until Rona puts their paint on sale?"

Marguerite smiled. "What we need is one of Amelia's coupons."

Amelia felt her cheeks grow hot as Marguerite explained about the coupons and the animals. Marguerite called it *Amelia's project*, and Amelia thought Rachel might think it was dumb.

But Rachel said, "No kidding? All those reptiles and stuff right across the street from me? That's so cool."

"Now," Marguerite said. "I just took zucchini cookies out of the oven before you got here. You're both invited to join me."

Rachel popped another bubble and said hastily, "Uh, I got another job to go see about."

"Me too," Amelia said. "I've got…um…lots of chores."

They left together.

"Hey," Rachel said. "I'm always looking for deals on nails and screws and paint. And I'd like to help save Winston. D'you think there are coupons for that kind of stuff?"

"I'll find some," Amelia said.

"Great." Rachel wrinkled her nose. "*Zucchini* cookies?"

✯ ✯ ✯

Bang! Bang! Bang!

Amelia was drifting to sleep when a loud popping noise jolted her awake. She met her mom in the hallway by the bathroom.

"Was that bullets?" she said.

"What?" Diane was holding a mug and her textbook. She had her first practical exam in two days, and she'd announced at supper that she was going to pull an all-nighter.

"Bullets. That noise. Someone was shooting at our house."

"Someone was *what*?"

"I'm serious. I think someone was trying to shoot us."

"Like who?"

"I don't know. The Mafia."

Diane snorted. Then she said, "You really are scared, aren't you, kiddo? I didn't hear anything. Are you sure it wasn't just a car backfiring?"

"It was way too loud. And I'm not scared. I just thought you should know."

"Come on."

Amelia followed her mom to the kitchen. Beaker gave a wolf whistle from his cage in the corner. Amelia and Diane burst out laughing at the same time.

"You're definitely a lady's man, Beaker," Diane said. "But you're supposed to be asleep. You'll wake up poor Mango, and he likes his beauty rest."

She set her book and mug on the counter and pulled back the curtain at the window. "Now look."

Amelia saw the dark shapes of a few parked cars and the Rachel's Renos van, but that was all.

"I did hear something," she said. "I guess it could have been a car backfiring. I'm not scared. I'm just telling you."

"Agreed," Diane said. "Now how about we make you some hot chocolate, and you can grab a book and keep me company in bed?"

Shivering, Amelia pulled her eyes away from the street. "Agreed."

THIRTY-THREE

Amelia slept in the next morning and missed the mailman.

"Was there anything for me?" she said sleepily as she plunked down at the kitchen table.

Diane turned off the blender. Mango was perched on one of her shoulders, Beaker on the other. She had a towel pinned around her neck to catch their messes. "Yes, there is. A letter from England. It says it's from—"

"ENGLAND! Are you kidding me?"

"No, I'm not kidding. And I've been dying for you to wake up so you could tell me—"

"WHERE IS IT?"

"On the table by the front door."

Amelia raced into the front hall and grabbed the pale-blue envelope. There was her name in beautiful handwriting, and a row of English stamps. And, in the top left corner, the words *Buckingham Palace, London, United Kingdom*.

Buckingham Palace!

She tore open the envelope. The paper was a matching pale blue with a fancy gold letterhead: *Her Majesty Queen Elizabeth II.*

Her heart pounding, Amelia read the letter.

Dear Amelia,

I receive a great deal of mail, but my staff brought your letter to me right away because they thought I would find it amusing.

I did not find your letter at all amusing! My heart goes out to Beaker and Winston and all the other animals you are trying to save.

I know you will be very disappointed, but I'm afraid a donation from me is not the answer to your problems. I admire your efforts in writing to all those celebrities, but I wonder if you are on the right track. Look around you, Amelia. The solution may be closer than you think.

Good luck in your endeavours.

Sincerely,
HM Queen Elizabeth II

Amelia's hopes crashed around her. Queen Elizabeth wasn't sending money. Not any! And what did she mean, *the solution may be closer than you think*?

She couldn't mean the pickle jar. There was only sixty-five dollars in it after Duke had taken out fifteen dollars for a bottle of Robitusson for Zak. Maybe another twenty bucks coming from Jordan, who was enthusiastically using his second set of cat coupons now, and another five bucks if Mick ever paid up (*I knew you couldn't trust him*, Liam had said when Amelia told him she had been back to the house twice, and Mick and the Mustang were never there). She'd been hunting, but she couldn't find one single coupon for paint or nails or anything that Rachel might use. And who knew if she was ever going to see Strawberry again?

Amelia had forced Duke to tell her how much the stronger drug for Winston was going to cost. Eight hundred bucks!! At this rate, she would have to find thousands of coupons!

She read the letter again, fighting back her disappointment. Queen Elizabeth's advice didn't make sense, and Amelia could tell she wasn't going to change her mind.

But still.

A *real* letter from Queen Elizabeth. Sent to *her*, Amelia.

"That's not really from Buckingham Palace, is it?" Diane called out.

"I'll tell you everything, Mom. But first I gotta call Roshni and Liam."

✵ ✵ ✵

"Let me see this," Liam said.

Roshni and Liam had rushed over, and they were all in Amelia's room. The first thing Roshni had done was accuse Amelia of keeping secrets again. *Sorry*, Amelia had said, but she was too excited to really care.

She produced the blue envelope now, with the letter tucked safely inside.

Liam examined the front of the envelope and then flipped it over. Then he took the letter out and read it aloud.

"This is so amazing," Roshni said. "She actually wrote to you. Omigod, I am so jealous."

Liam snorted. "Of what? This? You don't think this is real, do you?"

"It's real," Amelia said. "Look at the stamps. Those are real English stamps."

"And she signed it," Roshni said. "*HM Queen Elizabeth*. Whatever *HM* means."

"Her Majesty," Amelia and Liam said together.

"See?" Roshni said. "That proves it. Right, Amelia? And it's handwritten. If it was a fake, someone would have done it on a computer."

"What kind of logic is that? And it doesn't prove anything." Liam's voice rose an octave. "You girls are so gullible. Anybody could have written this letter."

"What about the English stamps?" Amelia persisted.

"Okay," Liam said. "I agree it came from England. There is a microscopic possibility it came from someone in Buckingham Palace. Maybe…her maid or her footman or someone. But there's no way Queen Elizabeth wrote this."

"Why not?" Roshni said.

"Because Queen Elizabeth doesn't write to kids she doesn't even know, that's why not! She's, like, BUSY!"

"But she could," Amelia said. "You have to admit she could."

"No way. It would just be too weird."

"Queen Elizabeth does weird things," Roshni said. "Look what she did at the Olympics. She parachuted into the stadium."

"That wasn't Queen Elizabeth!" Liam was practically shouting now.

"Okay," Amelia said. "You don't have to believe it, but I do."

"I know," Roshni said. "We can take it to the police station and ask them to dust it for fingerprints."

"What? Like Queen Elizabeth is on the FBI's Most Wanted list? Roshni, do you know how *anything* works?"

Amelia was tired of arguing. "I'll make you a bet, Liam. Your old iPod if I can prove this is real."

"And what will I get?" Liam said. "When I win?"

Amelia thought. "My entire set of Harry Potter books."

Liam's parents didn't approve of witchcraft, and Liam had been forced to read Harry Potter at the library.

"Deal," he said.

THIRTY-FOUR

Roshni came back the next morning to examine the letter. Amelia slumped in her beanbag chair, and Roshni flopped on the bed.

"When are you going to write back?" Roshni said.

Amelia hadn't thought of that. "I don't know. What would I say?"

"For starters, ask her about her great-grandchildren."

"Who?"

"William and Kate's kids! Queen Elizabeth probably adores them."

"Oh, right," Amelia said. "I don't know. It's not like she said to write back. She sounded kind of final."

"So? Do it! You and Queen Elizabeth could be pen pals! How awesome is that?"

Amelia couldn't help laughing. "We're not going to be pen pals!"

"Why not? You could ask her for her email address. That would be a lot easier."

"Forget it."

"Come on. We can ask her to say hi to Kate and William for us!"

Amelia groaned.

✻ ✻ ✻

Amelia gave Winston his fourth dose of tetracycline.

He was living on water that she squirted into his mouth and was mostly asleep.

She sat beside his pen.

Please, please, please get better.

✻ ✻ ✻

"What are *you* doing in here?" Amelia said the next morning when she came back to check on Winston.

Mick was leaning against a wall in the reptile room, his arms full of King Kong. "What does it look like I'm doing? Checking up on you to make sure you weren't lying about the animals."

"Did Duke say you could hold King Kong?"

"No. I just kinda got lost and wandered in here by mistake."

"Ha-ha, very funny. Did you bring the money?"

Mick saluted. "In the pickle jar, ma'am. Ten bucks."

He put King Kong back in his tank. "I'd give anything for a snake like this."

Amelia ignored him. She crouched down beside Winston's pen. Sleeping again.

Mick crouched beside her. "Is there anything I can do? To help?"

"No." Amelia's eyes blurred with tears. "There's nothing anyone can do."

Mick and Amelia set up a bin with Cheerios and honey for a new batch of wax worms that Duke had bought with money from the pickle jar. They only cost five dollars, but she was worried. The money in the pickle jar was growing so slowly, and she didn't think there would ever be enough for the drug.

"They look like maggots," Mick said when they dropped the white worms into their new home.

"But they're not," Amelia said. "They have legs and mouths, and maggots don't. They'll eat the honey, and then they'll make cocoons. And then they'll turn into moths. The moths don't eat anything because they don't have a mouth. They'll lay eggs and then die. And then there'll be more wax worms. Maybe seven or eight hundred."

"You know all that?" Mick said. "And who gets to eat these tasty morsels?"

"Apollo, Kilo, Oliver, the fire-bellied toads and Nate the tomato frog."

Mick made a smacking noise. "Oh, yum."

✿ ✿ ✿

In the afternoon Jordan came by the apartment, carrying a large glass aquarium.

"I used to keep fish," he told Amelia and Gabriella, who were couponing at the kitchen table. "Don't need it anymore."

"Duke is not here right now, but he will be so happy," Gabriella said.

Jordan set the tank on the counter. "Okay if I have a quick peek at Winston?"

Amelia took him into the reptile room. "He's asleep," she whispered.

She gave Jordan a quick tour of the other reptiles. Then she took him into the living room to see Mary, who was clinging upside down to the mesh on the top of her tank, Zak and Lysander, Georgia and the ferrets.

"I gotta get to the gym," Jordan said finally. "I'll see you guys later."

"See you," Gabriella said. "And thanks again."

Amelia sat down at the table and then leaped to her feet. She raced after Jordan and caught up to him on the street. "Wait a sec!"

She gave him a coupon for Whiskas cat food.

Jordan gave her a thumbs-up.

THIRTY-FIVE

"We're having a car wash," Amelia said. "Tomorrow, starting at five so we can get the people coming home from work."

"We are?" Liam said.

"Yup. To raise money for Winston."

"I've got my Mandarin lesson. And then Dad's taking me to get a new bike—"

"Mick's idea. Be there."

Amelia hung up before Liam could say another word, then called Roshni.

* * *

"Gabriella's going to give us some of Zak and Lysander's T-shirts for polishing rags," Amelia said. "And Mick says he's got tons of Turtle Wax."

Amelia and Roshni were kneeling on the living-room floor, making a sign on a piece of cardboard. Amelia used a fat felt pen to print *CAR WASH* in huge black letters, with an arrow underneath, and Roshni filled in the letters with red, orange and purple.

Roshni had thought up the sign and come over first thing in the morning to help make it. "We'll take turns standing on Hastings Street," she said. "We'll get tons of people."

"Marguerite's got a hose we can use," Amelia said.

"What about buckets and sponges?"

Amelia thought for a moment. "Rachel."

Roshni went home just before lunch, and Diane took Amelia shopping at the Lougheed Mall.

"Mother-daughter quality time," she said. "I want you to try on a few things that you'd like for your birthday."

Amelia picked out jeans with bleach streaks and a purple jacket, and Diane said, "You'll have to pretend to be surprised when I give them to you." Then she bought Amelia three tank tops, red, lime green and pink, to wear right away.

"Now. How about lunch at the Cactus Club for a treat?"

☆ ☆ ☆

When they were settled at their table and had been served, Diane said, "Amelia, there's something I want to tell you."

Amelia peered at her mother over her plate of calamari. "You've met a guy. You're crazy about him and you're getting married and you're putting me in foster care."

Diane grinned. "Be serious. Your dad and I are having dinner tomorrow. Just to talk. We thought it would be nicer for you if we could start being civil with each other again."

Amelia was silent for a moment. Then she said, "Any chance you might get back together?"

"No, sweetie. No, no. Even if Dad wanted to, I don't."

"You don't?"

"No."

"Oh."

"Anyway, he's got a baby now. He can't just…well, abandon that family now and come back to us."

"Right," Amelia said.

But inside she thought, He *could* if he really wanted to.

When they got home, Amelia went straight down to Duke and Gabriella's. The triplets' stroller was parked by the door. Strawberry and Gabriella were sitting at the kitchen table with cups of tea.

Amelia's mouth dropped open. "What happened? I mean, you look amazing, Strawberry. Your hair is gorgeous!"

"We put in some highlights to perk up her natural strawberry blond color," Gabriella said. She winked at Amelia.

Strawberry's cheeks turned pink. "I just came over with the money, and we started talking and—"

She burst into tears.

"*Mon dieu!*" Gabriella said. "You will ruin the makeup." She leaped to her feet and grabbed a piece of paper towel. "Here, pat your face with this."

Strawberry patted and sniffed and then gave them both a watery smile.

"I mean it—you really look beautiful," Amelia said.

"Thanks to Gabriella," Strawberry whispered. She showed Amelia her nails, which were silvery blue.

Gabriella shrugged. "I need to keep practising so that when I find a better job, I will be ready. I am going to specialize in complete makeovers."

"Where are the babies?" Amelia said.

"In there." Gabriella pointed to the living room.

Amelia peeked in the door. Duke and the triplets were fast asleep on the couch. Duke was snoring.

"He is a…what do you call it?" Gabriella said when Amelia came back.

"A natural," Amelia said.

THIRTY-SIX

"**D**on't even think about leaning that bike against my car," Mick said.

"You think I want Mustang germs on my brand-new Raleigh, dude?" Liam said.

"What took you so long?" Amelia called. "We've done three cars already!"

Mick was polishing a green hatchback while the owner, a man in a suit, leaned against a tree and read a newspaper. Duke was spraying mud off a silver SUV, and Amelia and Roshni were washing Simon's van. Simon was inside, his seat tipped back and the window open so he could call out suggestions.

"Hey, Liam," he said. "The girls have missed a bit of the back fender. And Roshni! A little more elbow grease, please!"

Simon rolled up the window just in time to miss Roshni's sponge. He made faces at them through the suds.

Liam lowered his bike to the grass.

"Is the sign still there?" Roshni said. She and Amelia had made two signs in the end—the big one, which they ended up taping to a streetlight on Hastings (after a fierce argument over which one of them had to stay at Hastings and hold it), and a smaller one with just an arrow, tacked to a telephone pole at the end of their block.

"Yup," Liam said. He waved his arms wildly as a red Mini turned up the street. "I'll direct traffic," he said as the car pulled up behind Simon's van.

"Forget it!" Roshni said. "Grab a sponge!" She beamed at the woman stepping out of the Mini. "Ten dollars for a wash. Special deal on Minis tonight. We throw the polishing in for free!"

Sudsy water pooled on the street and ran down the gutter. Most people wanted a quick slosh with sponge and hose and skipped the Turtle Wax. Amelia kept track of the number of cars. Jordan's blue Honda Civic was number seven. Marguerite's red Ford Fiesta was number ten, and the Rachel's Renos van was number twelve. Rachel pitched in to help and then insisted on giving a five-dollar tip. Amelia had brought the pickle jar, and by car number fourteen it was overflowing with bills.

There was one scary moment when Domenico showed up on his motorcycle. "Isn't that the Italian guy?" Roshni whispered. "Here comes trouble."

But Duke smiled and walked over and slapped Domenico on the back. "Hey, dude. Glad you made it.

These are the amazing kids I told you about. Amelia, Roshni and Liam."

"The loan!" blurted Amelia. "He'll pay you back! Honest!"

Domenico grinned. "He's paying me back with a snake. As soon as he gets in an interesting one, he's giving me a call. Now, how are you at polishing chrome?"

At seven thirty, Gabriella arrived, dressed in her salon clothes—a short black skirt and high-heeled sandals. By then things had slowed down. The last car had been fifteen minutes ago, and Amelia was secretly glad. Her arms were aching, and her fingers had shriveled up like raisins. She glanced around for Roshni, who was sitting on the curb, listening to Liam's new iPod.

Mick was showing Liam the Mustang's engine, and Duke was rolling up the water hose when a gleaming silver car that looked familiar glided up the street and pulled over. Amelia frowned. Where had she seen it before?

A man and a woman in a sari stepped out of the car. The East Indian couple from next door!

"Your car is so clean already," Amelia said.

The man smiled. "But I have a feeling this is for a good cause, so we'd like to participate. I'm Kamal Pawar, and this is my wife, Namita. I believe we're neighbors."

"I've been awful about coming over to meet you," Namita said. "Life just gets too busy. You've been there quite a few months now."

"Almost a year," Amelia said. She introduced everybody and then told Kamal and Namita about Winston and the other animals while Mick put a little extra shine on their car with some Turtle Wax.

"The coupon idea," Namita said. "That's brilliant. I'm always too lazy to look for myself."

"I'll bring some coupons over tomorrow," Amelia promised, "and you can pick out what you want."

Something landed *splat* in the middle of her back. She spun around.

"Wet-sponge fight!" yelled Liam.

✵   ✵   ✵

"Three hundred and twenty bucks," Duke said. "You guys are incredible."

Amelia, Duke, Gabriella, Simon, Liam, Roshni and Mick crowded around the kitchen table, dripping, while Diane sliced pieces of peach pie and Marguerite handed them out. Duke had dumped all the bills and coins out of the pickle jar, and they had counted it twice, just to make sure.

"That's a lot of money," Duke said.

But it's not enough, Amelia thought. She fought back a pang of disappointment and nibbled at the edge of her pie, listening to Gabriella talk about the apartment in Port Moody.

"Simon took us there this morning, and we are putting down a deposit tomorrow." Gabriella frowned. "It is a shame we are moving just when Rachel said she would build us some shelves in the reptile room. And the apartment, of course, is not perfect. There are marks on the ceiling from water, so I am thinking it will leak in the rain, and there is a strange smell coming out of the bathroom taps, and the landlord has a problem with booze. I have never seen so many empty wine bottles. But"—she flashed one of her dazzling smiles—"he is happy to have the animals."

Diane frowned.

After everybody had left, Diane disappeared while Amelia rinsed the pie plates and put them in the dishwasher. When she was finished, she went to her bedroom. She searched under the beanbag chair for the envelope with the phone number for the house in Langley. If Duke and Gabriella had to move, they should move somewhere good.

She put the envelope on her dresser and then sat on the edge of her bed, sorting through her stack of coupons. She tried to decide which ones Kamal and Namita might like. Their car had been spotless, so she figured they were into cleaning. She made a pile with Lysol spray, Arm & Hammer laundry detergent, Mr. Clean Magic Eraser, Febreze and Nellie's dryer balls. She didn't hear her mother come back.

"There," Diane said, standing in her doorway. "That's done."

"What's done?"

"I've told Duke and Gabriella they're not going anywhere."

Amelia leaped up, her coupons flying everywhere. Her heart soared. "They can stay? Like, for good? You really mean that?"

"Yes, I do."

"What made you change your mind? Was it that crummy apartment? Or was it Beaker and Mango? That was my idea."

"Nothing *made* me change my mind. I don't know why you say things like that. I changed it myself. I do have—"

"An open mind," Amelia said, beaming.

THIRTY-SEVEN

The next morning, Duke stood in the kitchen doorway in an old pair of sweatpants, his face unshaven and drawn.

"I've got some bad news," he said.

Amelia was swirling maple syrup on her stack of blueberry pancakes. She froze, watching the syrup sink into a pool in the middle.

"Sit down," Diane said. "I've made too many pancakes—"

"I'm not hungry," Duke said. "But thanks all the same."

"It's Winston, isn't it?" Amelia's words tumbled out in a rush. "He's getting way worse. He needs that drug—"

"He died."

Diane put down her fork. "Oh no."

"Sometime last night, I think. Or maybe early this morning. When I went in to check on him, he was gone."

"He can't be dead," Amelia said. "We were trying so hard." The back of her eyelids ached. She closed her eyes tightly, but tears squeezed through, dripping onto her pancakes.

"I am so sorry," Diane said. "If you could have got that drug, would it have saved him?"

"I don't know. It was a long shot. Winston was very sick. I think his kidneys failed him at the end."

"It's not fair." Amelia pushed away her plate of pancakes. She would choke if she swallowed one bite.

"Winston was suffering," Duke said quietly. "And now he's not. And Amelia, I want you to pick a place to bury him."

Fresh tears flooded Amelia's cheeks. She felt her mom's arms wrap around her shoulders.

When she could trust herself to talk, she said, "In Marguerite's garden."

✡ ✡ ✡

"It's called Moondance," Marguerite said. "It's one of my favorite roses. Smell one, Amelia."

Amelia put her nose almost inside one of the frothy, creamy-white flowers. It had a wonderful spicy smell. "Can we bury him here?" she said to Duke. "Right beside this rose bush?"

"It's a perfect spot," Duke agreed.

Marguerite gave Duke a shovel. Diane, Gabriella and Marguerite watched while Duke dug a deep hole. Amelia couldn't bear to look. She knelt beside the cardboard box on the grass. Winston was inside, wrapped in a soft green towel.

Duke had asked Amelia if she wanted to see Winston, and she had cried harder and said no. Now she changed her mind. She pulled back the corner of the towel. "He looks peaceful," she breathed.

Duke put down the shovel. "Ready?"

Amelia carefully folded the towel back around the tortoise. "Ready."

✮ ✮ ✮

"It's time for me to steal Amelia," Duke said.

"Just make sure you bring her back before midnight," Diane said, "or the bus will turn into a pumpkin."

"We're walking," Duke said.

Diane gave Amelia a hug. "Have fun, Cinderella."

"Where are we going?" Amelia said when they got outside.

"It's a surprise," Duke said.

"Does Mom know?"

"Yeah."

"Then why can't—"

"Shush."

They walked for twenty minutes, through neighborhoods Amelia had never been in before. She loved walking in the dark. Duke carried a flashlight, but he kept it turned off, because there was enough light from the streetlights. She also liked that they didn't talk. She wanted to think about Winston.

Then Duke turned onto the street in front of an elementary school. He flicked on the flashlight. "We're going around the back."

They walked across a playground, past the dark shapes of a climbing jungle and teeter-totters and onto a grassy playing field. Amelia stumbled on the bumpy ground, and Duke shone the flashlight in front of their feet.

"Okay," he said when they got to the far edge of the field. "There's a little hilly place where we can sit."

In the beam from the flashlight, Amelia could see smooth black water just below them, with tall reeds growing in the middle. She sat on the ground beside Duke and pulled her knees up to her chin. Duke turned the flashlight off.

"How did you find this place?" she whispered. She somehow felt she *should* whisper. She still wasn't sure why they were there, but it had the feeling of a great adventure.

"I thought I'd found a shortcut home from the gas station," Duke whispered back. "Turned out I was wrong. But I found this pond. Right in the middle of the city. There's a little creek that runs into it. Neat, huh? Now let's be quiet and listen."

Somewhere a dog barked, and she could hear the distant sound of traffic. Amelia concentrated.

And then she heard it. A hoarse, gravelly sound that made her jump.

"What is it?" she said.

"A frog," Duke said. "He was here last time too."

Duke was very still beside her. Amelia made herself keep still too. The frog kept up a steady croaking, and she thought it was the coolest sound she had ever heard. The cars and the barking dog disappeared, and she felt like they were a million miles away, in the middle of a jungle or a swamp.

She could tell that the frog was close, maybe right in front of them.

"Why is it croaking?" she said in a low voice.

"Looking for a mate or telling other male frogs to stay away. Or maybe he's telling us it's going to rain. Some tropical frogs do that."

"Like a weather forecast," Amelia said. She loved the croaking sound. Part of her wished she could see the frog, but it was more mysterious this way.

Then there was silence, with just the faint whisper of a breeze through leaves, and she shivered.

"Cold?" Duke said.

"No."

"Me neither. Was that the first time you've heard a wild frog?"

"Yeah."

"Nice."

Amelia thought of the fire-bellied toads and Nate the tomato frog and felt sad. "I wish Nate and the toads could be wild," she said. "And Mary and Kilo and Apollo and Oliver. Oh, and Pinecone too. And Bill and the snakes. Everybody."

"I wish they could too. But they probably came from pet stores and wouldn't know how to survive. We could never just set them free. Look what happened to Winston."

"I know they couldn't live here. Only in the rainforest or desert or wherever they came from."

They were quiet for a moment.

Then Duke said, "One of these days I'm going to go to the Galapagos Islands."

"Where's that?"

"In South America, near Ecuador. You can take boat tours there. It's kind of a wildlife paradise. There are iguanas, lizards, geckos and a tortoise called the Galapagos tortoise that can get to be 150 years old. And tons of birds. All living wild. I'd love to see it."

"I'm going to go there too," Amelia said.

"Well," Duke said, getting to his feet and stretching, "I think that old frog is done for tonight."

Amelia stood up too. "The money in the pickle jar. It was all for nothing, wasn't it?"

"What?" Duke said. "No way! We've got all the other animals to look after. They depend on us. And because of you, everyone in the neighborhood wants to help."

He grinned. "Mick was actually excited about cleaning up ferret poop yesterday. You can't give up on me now, Amelia."

"I won't."

THIRTY-EIGHT

Your Majesty,

I'm sorry I never wrote back, but I have been very busy raising money and looking after the animals. I thought you would want to know that Winston got very sick and died. I am NOT blaming you. There was a drug we needed, but we couldn't get it in time, so even if you had sent the money, Winston would have died. Duke said the drug was a long shot, but I still feel angry and really, really sad. I didn't get what you said in your letter about the answer to my problems being closer than I thought, but now I think I do. The celebrities never even wrote back, but there are tons of neat people in my neighborhood who are all trying to help. So thank you for your advice. Roshni wants you to say hi to Kate and William for her.

Respectfully yours,
Amelia

THIRTY-NINE

oshni took a small box off her dresser and handed it to Amelia. "Happy birthday!"

"*Splat Washables*?" Amelia said, reading the side of the box. "*Easy to Apply Hair Color?*"

"It's called Totally Red. It's gonna be totally you."

Amelia studied the photograph of a woman who looked like a movie star on the front of the box. "I don't think so."

"Come on. Just streaks. And it washes out. It's not half as scary as what I did."

Scary was a good word to describe Roshni's wild hair, Amelia thought. She opened the box and took out a skinny tube and a brush that looked like one of Gabriella's mascara brushes, only bigger. She peered inside the empty box. "No instructions."

"On the back of the box," Roshni said.

Amelia turned the box over. "*Squeeze a small amount of color onto applicator brush,*" she read. "*Comb through hair from roots to ends.*"

"Easy," Roshni said.

"*Must not be used for dyeing eyelashes or eyebrows.*"

Roshni snorted and Amelia giggled.

"It says *Rebellious Colors,*" Amelia said.

"Right. You're twelve today. It's about time you rebelled."

✷ ✷ ✷

They stood side by side in front of the bathroom mirror. Fluorescent red, brilliant pink, dazzling turquoise.

"We look awesome," Roshni said.

"We do," Amelia agreed. "Let's go show Gabriella!"

"Now?"

"Now. Come on!"

✷ ✷ ✷

Roshni was acting weird. She kept peeking at her watch the whole way back to Amelia's.

"You're walking too fast," she said as they turned the corner onto Amelia's block. "Slow down."

"Do you think it's going to rain?" she said a minute later.

Amelia glanced at the gray clouds piling up in the sky. "Probably."

Roshni groaned. Then she lingered a whole ten minutes in front of Jordan's house, fussing over the cats, who were all outside.

When they got to the door of the apartment, Roshni looked at her watch one last time. "Okay. You can knock."

"Thanks for your permission." Amelia knocked and then opened the door and shouted, "It's us!"

Gabriella must have been standing right next to the door. "Your hair! *Superbe!*" She hugged Amelia. "Happy birthday! You must show Duke your hair. He is in the living room."

Gabriella and Roshni exchanged looks, and Roshni started to giggle. Weird, thought Amelia again.

She stepped through the living-room door. Something was draped across the one little window, and there were no lights on. She stopped, confused. Then a chorus of voices shouted, "HAPPY BIRTHDAY!"

The lights flicked on and Amelia stared at a sea of faces. Duke, her mom, Liam, Marguerite, Jordan, Rachel, Strawberry and the triplets, Mick, Kamal, Namita, Simon, Jeannie and Frank. And, *mon dieu*, the Mafia guy, Domenico! Everybody was grinning.

"You said you didn't want a party," Diane said, "but you were outvoted."

"I knew! I knew!" Roshni yelped. "It was my job to keep you busy. Tell me you didn't suspect."

"I didn't." How could she ever have suspected this?

"*Bon anniversaire!*" Gabriella said.

And then Liam called out something that sounded like *shung ruh kwy luh.* He shrugged. "That's *happy birthday* in Mandarin."

"The barbecue's in the back of my van," Simon said. "Let's fire it up and get this party started."

Simon and Jordan rolled the barbecue onto the front lawn, and Rachel, Strawberry and Gabriella set out wieners, hamburger patties, buns and bowls of chips on a card table. Liam and Mick tied helium balloons (which had been hidden in Duke and Gabriella's bathroom) to the lawn chairs (hidden in the backyard.) Diane set her iPod station on the front step and turned up the volume on *The Beatles: Greatest Hits*.

When Amelia ran into their kitchen to get ketchup and mustard, she spotted a huge white bakery box on the counter. She peeked inside. *Happy Birthday Amelia* was written in gooey pink letters on a round white cake. From their cages in the corner of the kitchen, Beaker whistled and Mango gave a screech. Amelia was pretty sure they were saying "Happy Birthday" too.

Halfway through her third hot dog, a red minivan drove slowly down their street and pulled over in front of the house. She could see two faces with blond pigtails peering out at her. Dad had brought the twins.

She walked over to the van slowly. Her dad got out.

"New van?"

"Secondhand. Or maybe thirdhand." Her dad's eyes drifted over to the front yard, where Strawberry, Diane and Domenico were dancing on the grass to "A Hard Day's Night," and he looked a little confused. "It's quite a gathering you have here." Then he added, "Amelia, there's something I wanted to talk to you about. I…uh…wanted to tell you myself."

Amelia was pretty sure she knew what it was. "Not on my birthday."

"It's your birthday? Today?"

"Yup. And this is my party."

Her dad's face sagged. "I can't believe I forgot."

He dug in his pocket and pulled out his wallet. He gave Amelia two twenty-dollar bills. "I know it's not that camp you wanted to go to so badly, but maybe you can buy yourself some new clothes."

"I don't want to go to camp anymore anyway," Amelia said. "I've got too much to do around here. And thanks, Dad. That's great." She stuffed the money in the pocket of her jeans. As soon as she got a chance, it was going straight to the pickle jar.

"Do you want to join us? The twins—I mean, Kelsey and Kaitlin could have a hot dog. And there's watermelon."

Her dad pulled out his cell phone and shut it off. "You bet I do!"

✵ ✵ ✵

The first raindrops started after Amelia had blown out her candles. Everyone carried their plates of cake inside the house, crowding into the living room.

Duke made an announcement. "There's a brand-new beauty salon opening up next month, and they've hired Gabriella! Full time!"

"Do not forget the rest," Gabriella said. "Diane and I are going into business together on the weekends. Massages and makeovers. Two for the price of one!"

"Can I get a coupon for that?" Jordan called out.

"Well, Amelia," Marguerite said. "Did you know you're sharing your birthday with George, the future king of England?"

"It's Prince George's birthday today?" Roshni screeched. "And I forgot?"

Her eyes went straight to the TV. "It might be on the news. Please, please, please, everyone. Just for a minute."

Liam groaned loudly, but there were a lot of royalists at the party. In the end, everyone congregated in front of the TV.

Roshni grabbed the remote and flipped through channels until suddenly Queen Elizabeth filled the screen, a corgi on her lap and a sea of microphones in front of her.

"I can only say how delighted I am with my great-grandchildren," she said. "George and his sister and their parents are spending the day with Kate's parents. I ask that you all respect their privacy."

"Are you a doting great-granny?" a man's voice said. "Planning on spoiling the birthday boy with gifts?"

"Grannies are permitted to spoil their great-grandchildren," Queen Elizabeth said. "I've sent a few gifts. My favorite is a squishy stuffed tortoise called Winston."

"*Mon dieu!*" Gabriella said. "Did I hear right? Winston?"

"She must have named it after Winston Churchill," Liam said. "He was a famous prime minister."

But he was shouted down by everyone in the room.

"Liam," Amelia said with a huge grin. "You owe me an iPod!"

ACKNOWLEDGMENTS

This book would never have been written without my nephew Michael Ames and his wife, Bianca. Their passion for rescuing abused or abandoned animals is amazing. Every animal under their care, no matter how small, receives attention and love. I want to thank Michael and Bianca for welcoming me into their home to meet their animals and for their endless patience in answering my questions. I would also like to thank my editor, Amy Collins, who was so enthusiastic about the story and made the editing fun, and the whole team at Orca, who are so supportive of my writing. My mother, June, and my sister Janet, as always, listened to many drafts and gave invaluable suggestions. My wonderful husband, Larry, makes it possible for me to have the time to write.

BECKY CITRA is the author of over twenty books for children, ranging from early chapter books to novels for young adults. She taught in elementary schools for over twenty-five years and began writing for children in 1995. Becky's books have been shortlisted for and won many awards, including the Red Cedar Award, the Diamond Willow, the Silver Birch and the Sheila A. Egoff Children's Literature Prize. She lives in Bridge Lake, British Columbia. For more information, visit www.beckycitra.com.